FRACTURED ERA: LEGACY CODE BOOK ONE

LEGACY CODE

AUTUMN KALQUIST

Diapason Publishing

For my husband, Juan.
For believing in me and supporting me, even when times get tough.
For all the evenings you come home tired, yet still find the energy to be an amazing dad.
And for saying, "You have to do what makes you happy."

CHAPTER ONE

Era huddled against the wall and pressed her hands to her ears, blocking out the piercing sirens. The emergency lights cast a red glow over the rest of the colonists in the stairwell. One step above her, a mother held a young boy, his eyes wide in fear. Era dropped her hands and clamped them over the gentle swell of her belly.

Where was Dritan now? First shift was over. He'd be done working. *Safe.*

Today they'd finally find out if their baby had the Defect. She'd be late for her appointment, but it couldn't be helped. The entire ship was on lockdown.

Was it a fire? A hull breach? Another uprising? Era shivered. No. She would not let herself imagine all the things that could have gone wrong. The *Paragon* was the safest ship in the fleet. Whatever the problem was, they'd have it under control.

But a maintenance crew might be called during an emergency like this. A maintenance crew like the one Dritan was on.

Era stared at the panel across from her and began to count the rivets, one by one, pushing her terror down. When she ran out of rivets to count, she started over.

Then the sirens cut out, and the emergency lights shut off.

"All clear." A voice blared from the speakers above the landing. "You may now return to your duties."

Era blinked in the silence and gripped the handrail. The flickering yellow light of the dying lume bar above the landing cast strange shadows over the colonists. The young boy broke into sobs. His mother reprimanded him, but he didn't stop.

Era stood, shaking, and walked up the stairs. The *Paragon* had dedicated all of level four to Medical. She kept going until she reached it. Several colonists waited in front of medlevel's doors. A whir sounded, and the locks disengaged.

As the doors slid open, a group of colonists exited and ran up the stairs. Light blue suits, the helix and triquetra patch on their sleeves. Medics. Era's stomach clenched. Which sector had Dritan's crew worked today?

The sting of disinfectant burned her throat as she entered the waiting area. She surveyed the space, trying to ignore the sick feeling in the pit of her stomach. A few people waited on the worn metal benches.

Dritan wasn't one of them.

A line of clerks sat at stations against the wall, and Era headed for the one marked *Population Management*.

A young brunette clerk, face drawn, sat up straighter behind the high counter as Era approached.

Era swiped her shift card across the stationary's scanner, and the large black box beeped in response, verifying her check-in.

The clerk twisted her wrist to the right, and her small transparent eyepiece darkened, taking on a reflective quality. She splayed her fingers wide to bring up an interface only she

3

could see. "Era Corinth?" She stood. "Follow me."

Era glanced back at the doors. Dritan had promised he'd be here—that she wouldn't have to face this alone. But he was too late. She wiped her damp palms down the coarse fabric of her suit and hurried after the clerk.

"Do you know what happened?" Era asked as they entered the wide corridor behind the waiting area.

The clerk stiffened and kept her gaze straight ahead. "I'm sure they'll tell us if we need to know."

Era swallowed and tried to focus on the route they were taking.

It'd been hard to get used to the maze of corridors on this ship. She'd grown up on one of the smaller manufacturing ships in the fleet, the *London*. Her home, like every other deka, only had a single medcubic. But the *Paragon* was the fleet's flagship, ten times the size of the largest deka. When you needed the best medical care, you applied to come here.

The clerk stopped at a cubic and ran her shift card across the scanner. The door opened, but Era hesitated. What if Dritan was

4

injured, or worse? He'd never miss this. What had kept him?

The speakers in the ceiling crackled. "Medics to medbay three. Medics to medbay three. All hands clear the entrance. Incoming casualties."

The clerk paled and gestured to the cubic. "The medic will be by soon."

Era steeled herself, her heart in her throat, and stepped into the small space.

A tattered exam table, two stools, curved cabinets anchored to the walls. It was nearly identical to the place where they'd removed her implant so she could get pregnant. But she'd never seen a machine like the one in the center of *this* medcubic.

The rusted panels were missing rivets, and a crack ran through the main holo interface. Had to be the genscanner. The *Paragon* had the only one in the fleet. The medic would use it to scan her womb, and they'd know right away if her baby had the Defect. Pain-free, unlike an amnio.

Era sat on a stool and pushed up the cuff of her suit. She traced the infinity symbol on her wrist. She'd gotten the left half, teardrop-shaped, when she turned twelve and became an apprentice. The right half stood out, its pigment darker. They'd completed her tattoo eleven months ago, the day she'd paired with Dritan.

An image of Dritan formed in her mind. His body battered and bloody. His chest, still. Once-bright hazel eyes staring blankly ahead, their spark gone. She squeezed her eyes shut. *Incoming casualties.*

After the sirens shut off, those medics had run *up* the stairs. Dritan's crew spent most of their time doing maintenance in the sublevels, didn't they? He'd be fine. He probably just got held up by the lockdown like she had.

The door slid open, and Era opened her eyes. An old woman with short, gray hair entered. The lines on her face made her look older than fifty—the right age to be a patient on medlevel, not a working medic.

The woman gave Era a tight smile, twisted her wrist, and her eyepiece darkened. With one finger, she tapped the air in front of her and opened her hand wide. "I'm Medic Faust. And you are...age seventeen, fifteen weeks pregnant..." Her lips parted, and her hand froze mid-gesture. "Era Corinth. Your husband's name is...?"

"Dritan Corinth."

"Corinth..." Medic Faust said, a strange edge in her voice. "From which deka?"

"The *London*." Era squeezed her hands tighter in her lap.

"Oh. Was he born there?"

Why did it matter? *I just want to get this over with.*

"No, actually. He was born on the *Meso*."

Medic Faust studied her and gave Era a small smile.

"Well." She turned to the genscanner and gestured. The machine hummed to life. "Unzip your suit to the waist, and lie down please. This will only take a minute."

Era's heart sped up. *Just get it over with.* Besides, the sooner this was over, the sooner she could find Dritan.

She unzipped her faded black suit with slow care. The zipper had already come away from it twice, and half the pockets had holes in them. It couldn't take many more repairs. If she lost it, she'd be down to one. It'd take months to work her way up the list and get a new suit from the *Vancouver*, the textile deka.

The cool air hit her skin, and she shivered, crossed her arms over her sore breasts, and

7

climbed onto the exam table. As she lay back, the cracked plastic stuck to her, prompting goosebumps to spring up along her arms.

The medic took several square patches from the cabinet and pressed one onto Era's bare belly. "Just a small charge."

A tiny shock rushed through Era, and she winced. Medic Faust frowned, peeled the patch off, and applied a second one. Another shock coursed through Era's body.

The medic made a fist to shut off the genscanner. "This is what happens when we don't get the parts we request. We'll have to do this the way the rest of the fleet does, I'm afraid." She lifted the patch from Era's abdomen and turned to the cabinet. "I'm sorry. I'm sure you were relieved to bypass the needle."

The medic carried a tray over and set it on the shelf next to the exam table.

The needle was huge.

"Amnio?" Era sat up, her stomach churning. "There's less risk with the scanner, isn't there?"

"Yes. A scan's safer than amnio, but—" she lifted the needle from the tray, "I've done this many, many times. Lie back, please."

Era settled back on the table. Experienced.

Probably the most experienced medic in the fleet.

Medic Faust placed a cold hand on her lower abdomen and pushed down, feeling for something. Era stared up at the lume bar in the ceiling and tried to keep her breathing even.

"A pinch, now."

Searing pain shot through Era, the shock of it worse than grabbing a glitching helio from the air barehanded.

"Hold still."

The needle quivered from where it had been plunged deep into her womb. The muscles in her abdomen seemed to seize up, and Era fought to keep still, trying not to imagine how deep the needle went.

Medic Faust twisted a tube onto the needle and pulled, drawing up clear liquid. After an agonizing minute, it was over, and the medic smoothed a bandage over the wound. She held the vial up to the light. "Good. We got enough. Your results should be back in about a week."

Era's hands shook as she zipped up her suit, and her stomach threatened to eject the quin gruel she'd eaten at first mess. Another week waiting for the answer.

"Medic Faust?" Era licked her lips. She should leave now and not ask, but she had to know. "What are the odds that my baby will—"

"Never call it that. It's a collection of non-sentient cells."

Era swallowed. "What are the chances the cells will have the Defect? Has anything changed?"

The medic pressed her lips together, and a dark look passed over her face. "Still fifty percent." She placed the vial on the tray and opened the door, not making eye contact. "You can check back in one week to schedule your follow-up."

Era mumbled her thanks and stepped into the corridor. She tried to ignore the dull ache in her womb.

Two women walked toward her, down the corridor. The clerk from population management and a young pregnant woman with dark skin. The size of the gentle rise beneath the woman's suit suggested her pregnancy was nearly as far along as Era's. The woman met Era's eyes and gave her a small nod.

The clerk opened the door to a cubic, and Era glimpsed an exam table and an array of scuffed and dented machines beyond.

"You'll be sedated," the clerk said. "When you wake up, it'll be gone, scraped clean. Easy and quick."

"Okay. Thank you," the woman said.

Era rested a hand over the throbbing spot on her belly and quickened her pace, retracing her steps to the waiting area.

Fifty percent. One in two.

One in two died, but that also meant one in two lived.

Even if she had to abort, they'd place her back in the lottery. There'd been more pregnancy approvals lately. They'd lost so many colonists on Soren. Balance needed to be restored.

If this..."collection of cells" had the Defect, she might get another chance. Why, then, didn't the thought make her feel better?

Era slowed as she reached the waiting area. A crowd had gathered. They stood in front of the benches, blocking her view. She inched around a few of the waiting patients and saw what they saw. Medics, rushing through the doors.

The first medics ran past Era, a stretcher between them, and she caught sight of a guard. He was unconscious, a mask and oxygen pack on his face.

The room tilted around Era, and her nausea intensified. A second pair of medics went by carrying another wounded guard. He had a blanket over his legs, the blue fabric soaked through in places. Blood dripped from the stretcher, leaving a trail of bright red dots that marked the tiles and extended back into the stairwell beyond.

The crowd waited, but no other medics came through the doors. Era pushed past the people in her way and hurried to the stairs. If nothing had happened to Dritan, he'd be waiting for her in their cubic. *Please be there.*

∞　∞

Era reached level one, home level for paired couples on the *Paragon*. Her heart pounded as she hurried past the long line of cubics.

A pair of maintenance workers lifted a panel from the wall and blocked her path. They'd stripped half the walls, exposing ancient components and bundles of wiring. A middle-aged tech ran diagnostics at the end of the corridor. From afar, he could've been her father working on the *London*. Before the accident.

A hard knot of fear expanded in Era's chest as she neared their cubic. It only took the swipe of her shift card and a quick glance to see the small space was dark. Empty.

Era leaned against the wall next to their door, eyes closed. The system would have shown she was scheduled for an appointment during midbreak. Someone would have found her, told her if Dritan had been in an accident. Wouldn't they have?

But no one had told her last time.

She had overheard Zephyr's father give the orders, and she'd rushed down the stairs, taking them two at a time, to the *London*'s sublevels.

The crowd had gathered in the jumpgate sector. The sector that stayed dormant for decades until the need for another gate arose.

Her father's body had lain mangled in a pool of his own blood, a red arc of it splattered across the machinery next to him.

No one noticed her standing there. No one except Dritan.

He'd recognized her as the lead tech's daughter and had pulled her away. She'd cried

13

in his arms, her tears mingling with the grease stains on his green sublevel suit.

He'd been there for her that day and every day after. They'd left the London to get away from the accidents, the random acts of violence, the terrorist threats, the deadly Soren work draft. If something had happened to him, if coming here had all been for nothing...

"Era."

Her breath caught, and she opened her eyes. Dritan strode down the corridor toward her, his expression grim. At the sight of him—his brown skin, the hazel eyes she could lose herself in—the pain in her chest vanished.

He drew her close and pressed his warm lips to hers. She melted into the intensity of his kiss, every muscle in her body relaxing.

"What happened?" she asked, her voice wavering.

"Let's talk in the cubic."

CHAPTER TWO

Era stepped into their living compartment and felt around for the helio. When her hand found the small, cool sphere, she tapped it and threw it into the air. It hovered next to her like a miniature metal-bound sun, bright streams of light emanating from it. After a moment, it flickered and began to bob.

The dying helio bounced off the wall, and Dritan grunted and snatched it from the air. He opened one of its small, curved panels, pulled out its charging prongs, and inserted them into the receptacle in the wall. The helio lit up again, pulsing every few moments to indicate it wasn't yet fully charged.

"Damn piece of kak. They better get us a new lume bar soon." He ran a hand through his tight black curls, pulling on them. "Did you—?"

"The scanner didn't work. The medic had to do an amnio, so we wait." Era clenched her hands into fists and studied Dritan's face. "Where were you? What happened? I was in the stairwell when the alarm went off. I was afraid you..."

Dritan took a few steps to the end of the cubic, grabbed their canteen from the shelf, and took a long drink. He sank down on the bunk and stared straight ahead. "There was a hull breach. My crew got called in to help with the evac."

Era lifted a hand to her chest and walked over to sit beside him. A hull breach. She'd been right to worry. Dritan's parents had both died during a botched hull repair. "What level?"

"Six. Executive sector."

Era clutched the stiff blanket under her. "Is the president...?"

"The president and board were in session, and their chamber locked down. I don't think there were any deaths. But there were some injuries before...before the breach got temp-sealed. Guards."

"I saw them come in on medlevel. What happened? I thought they scanned for hull damage a few months ago and fixed all the weak areas."

"They did."

"How could they miss this?"

Dritan bit his lower lip and twisted the canteen in his hands. "It wasn't missed. New panels were just installed in that sector."

"But if they were new..."

Dritan shifted on the bunk and leaned forward to set the canteen back on the shelf.

"I don't get it," Era said. "There shouldn't have been a breach in a new section of the hull."

Dritan shrugged, not meeting her gaze.

Era moved closer to him and laid a hand on his arm. "What are you not telling me?"

Dritan finally looked at her and hesitated, studying her face. "Some people are saying it might not have been an accident."

"Not an accident? What? Like..."

Like the breach that happened on the Oslo? Traitors had blown out a water tank, and it took the fleet months to recover. Era grew thirsty just remembering the way the canteen faucets had run dry at the end of it all. But the

17

Paragon was safe. Nothing like that had ever happened here.

Dritan grabbed Era's hand. "They're just jumping to conclusions. They don't know anything. Bunch of execs and guards with no experience in maintenance. Trust me. Everyone in maintenance thinks either the panels or the rivets were weak, or warped. That's all it would take."

"Weak metal? So...what? You think they'll blame this on the *London*?"

He drew up her chin and met her eyes. "I don't know, and I don't care. It's over."

"Yeah, unless they send your crew out to fix it. I don't know how you managed to avoid hull duty for so long, but let's hope your luck holds."

How *had* he managed to avoid hull duty?

He stiffened, but then his eyes brightened, and he raised his eyebrows. "Hey, maybe they'll send me to compost next. I'll bring the fine aroma of kak back to the cubic every night. You'll be ready to change my suit out for spacegear in no time."

She let out the breath she'd been holding and gave him a half-smile. "Guess I should watch what I wish for."

Dritan reached down and unzipped the pocket on his pant leg. He pulled out a folded square of pale green cloth. "Found this in textile recyc today."

Era took it. "Exec-standard bedding." She sighed. It was plush, soft, smooth. Only the most senior command level families got this bedding. Era used to go to Zephyr's cubic just to lie on her bunk.

"You know you can't keep this. It has to go back to recyc. We'll be in trouble if they catch us with it. And why'd you take it? It's just a scrap."

Dritan plucked the cloth from her hand and unfolded it, spreading it across his lap. He picked up one edge and wiped the soft material along Era's cheek. "It's not big enough for us, but it's just the right size—for someone smaller."

Era's chest lightened, and she pressed her lips together to suppress a smile. "Fine. Just...make sure you hide it."

Dritan grinned and set the scrap aside. He pulled her down onto the bunk and took her hand. He stroked her palm, and she stared at their distorted reflections in the metal ceiling.

If they got through these repairs, if they finished the jumpgate and jumped the fleet, if their baby was healthy and didn't have the Defect...if all that happened, life would be perfect, or as close as it ever could be. She'd live here on the flagship with her family, searching for a better world, far away from Soren.

Dritan squeezed her hand, three quick pulses. She rolled toward him, met his eyes, and squeezed his hand three times in return. *I. Love. You.*

A smile played across his full lips, and he brought her closer, laying both their hands over the swell of her belly.

Would their child have his dark skin or her lighter complexion? Any child of his would be beautiful. She snuggled closer.

Too many ifs. Too soon to think about this. *Just cells, Era.*

"It's probably almost second shift," Dritan said. "Shouldn't ya get going?"

Era groaned and sat up. "Yeah. I told Zephyr I'd meet her before shift."

"Well, I need to clean up and get to mess before it ends anyway. Just don't let her get you into any trouble."

Era leaned in and kissed him again. "I

was really worried about you."

"I'm okay, and you are too. Go on. I'll see you at last mess."

She got up, walked to the door, and hit the button. She held her breath, expecting it to jam like it always did, but this time it opened.

Era stepped into the corridor. Fumes from burnt plastic filled her lungs, and she coughed. The pair of workers she'd passed earlier argued in front of the source of the scent—a stretch of wall now marred by singed wires and blackened components.

Era breathed through her mouth until she reached the stairs. Dritan was safe *this* time and *this* hull breach had been temp-sealed, but how long would it be until the next thing went wrong?

∞   ∞

Era approached level six, and traffic in the main stairwell slowed to a crawl. Several guards stood outside the doors, blocking the landing. One spoke into his comcuff, and the others watched the passing colonists.

These were new guards. The deep blue fabric of their suits was unfaded, and the silver infinity symbols printed on each sleeve smooth and uncracked. The Paragon Guard had grown a lot in the ten months since Era had transferred here.

Her gaze fell to the nearest guard, to the pulse gun holstered at his belt, and the hairs on the back of her neck lifted. Zephyr's father had a few pulse guns on the bridge of the *London*, but she'd only seen them once. The day of the riots.

The *Paragon* hadn't rioted, though. The guards here had kept the people safe.

When she'd finished crossing the landing, she let out a breath and started up the next flight of stairs. The crowd thinned as she approached the observation deck.

Era swiped her card across the scanner, and when the system verified she had free shift, the doors slid open.

Soren loomed across the horizon, the swirling dark-red clouds of its atmosphere warning of the noxious air below.

The jumpgate hung off to the side of the planet. Only half the massive metal circle was complete—extra, unused parts still moored to the work ship.

Era forced herself to look away. That

22

thing was responsible for her father's death. But without it, they'd never be able to open a wormhole and jump the fleet to their next destination. They'd be stuck here forever.

The fleet had jumped five times since it'd fled Earth three hundred years ago, and each jump had, quite literally, been a leap of faith. Maybe their next one would land them in a system with a new Earth. There'd be no way to know until they got there.

After each jump, the fleet had traveled for decades to find a resource-rich planet to mine so they could repair their ships and build the next jumpgate. The planets they'd found had always been uninhabitable, had always been toxic like Soren.

She glanced again at the red planet and shuddered. Thousands of colonists had died mining it. The sooner they left this place, the better.

Era scanned the deck for Zephyr. It was nearly deserted this close to the end of midbreak.

Zephyr sat on one of the worn metal benches in front of the expanse. Long redblond hair cascaded down her back, and her hand moved rhythmically in front of her.

Era shook her head. Zephyr never would've used her handheld on the *London*'s observation deck. People would've swarmed her to get a look at the tech only the captain's daughter had personal access to.

No one even blinked an eye on the *Paragon*. Maybe it was because they seemed to have most of the fleet's ancient stockpile of handhelds at their disposal.

Zephyr made a fist, and a light melody began to play, her recorded vocals layered over it.

A straight line
from first breath to last.
This recycled air remembers
all the lies told in its past.

Sins of the father,
that's what they say.
That's how life goes,
what we're living today.

There's more than this; I feel it.
Drifting through
this useless existence.
Held down by artificial gravity.

Era sat on the bench and winced against the sharp pain that shot through her lower abdomen. Her pregnancy pains got worse every day.

Zephyr made a fist to shut the holo off and deactivated her eyepiece.

"I like it," Era said. "Kinda dark, but..."

A hint of a smile crossed Zephyr's lips. "Well, it's not done yet."

Her gaze flicked to Era's stomach.

"Scanner wasn't working. Had to get an amnio. That needle's a lot bigger than you'd think."

Zephyr grimaced. "I don't want to know. You hear what happened in executive?"

"Dritan's crew helped with the evac."

"Really." Zephyr looked over her shoulder at the deck and leaned closer. "Don't you think it's a little strange that the breach just happened to be in the same corridor where the president and board meet?"

Era shifted on the bench. "Dritan didn't mention that."

"What did he say?"

"Well...he said something might've been wrong with the panels. They were new."

Zephyr crossed her arms over her chest. "Yeah, I'd like to see them try to lay this on my father. The *London* hasn't failed a qual scan since we got here."

Era raised her brows. Zephyr defending her father? This was new.

The *London* had passed all its quality scans, but if Dritan thought it was the panels, it probably was. She opened her mouth to say so but clamped it shut.

Zephyr's light blue eyes had taken on a glassy sheen. She sniffed and angled her face away.

What could be bad enough to make her cry? Era hadn't seen her cry in years.

When they were seven or eight, Zephyr had talked Era into stealing tech gear to explore parts of the ship they couldn't get to on their own. But instead, they'd gotten locked in a storage cubic for an entire day.

They'd both cried in the dark, thirsty and scared, until someone found them. Zephyr had a half-truth ready, but Era blurted out the whole story, like usual. Zephyr had gotten the brunt of that punishment. Also like usual.

Zephyr looked at the empty deck again, lips pressed together, and faced Era. If there'd been tears, they were gone now. "I asked my mother about the jumpgate," she said. "Comms came during first shift."

Era straightened, one hand over her stomach. "She sent a message? Will it be done soon?"

"The jumpgate sector's been shut down. All the orders coming in are for panels."

"Maybe they need the panels to fix the ships—"

"No." Zephyr stood and walked to the viewing area. She drew her fingers along the glass, tracing Soren's barren landscape. "Almost all the incoming orders are for Soren."

The saliva evaporated from Era's mouth. "But...why? The president said the subcity was finished."

"They have to be expanding it," Zephyr said, her voice low. "Why else would they send everything down there?"

Expansion would mean drafting more workers, but how many more workers could the fleet really spare?

The *Paragon* was exempt from the work draft, but the dekas weren't. Maintenance crews from the sublevels had been drafted

27

first. Dritan would have been sent down if he'd turned eighteen on the *London*.

Maybe Zephyr's father wasn't the best, but he'd gotten Era and Dritan placements here and had probably saved Dritan's life. Mining was dangerous enough, but they had equipment for that. Carving a livable subcity through rocky soil on a planet riddled with quakes had proven even deadlier.

Era shook her head. "But why would they expand it? There's no reason—"

"Don't you see?" Zephyr said, drawing the words out. "We're never leaving Soren."

A loud laugh bubbled up from Era's throat, and she choked it back. The fleet hadn't traveled for three hundred years just to die out on a planet worse than the one they'd left. Soren wasn't the first resource-rich planet, and it wouldn't be the last. "That doesn't even make sense. They can't expect us to abandon our ships and settle here. We can't live down there."

"My parents have talked about it before," Zephyr said. "What if the fleet can't survive another jump? Our ships are falling apart."

"No one wants to stay here. The president will—"

28

"The president will what? Save us all? The president does what's good for the president."

"Don't say that." Era glanced over her shoulder to the empty deck.

To live and die on a planet where she'd never see the stars again—to raise a child surrounded by metal walls, no view of the beauty in space, no hope for a better world ahead...

The fleet would never stay here.

Era stood up. "Come on. We're gonna be late for shift. You need to stop at your bunk?"

Zephyr sniffed and didn't move. "No."

"If Mali catches you with outside tech again..."

"Then what?" Zephyr slid her handheld and eyepiece into a pocket on the leg of her suit and zippered it shut. "It's not like I use it in there. It's an idiotic rule." She strode toward the doors.

Era sighed and followed her. If Zephyr didn't learn to keep her mouth shut, she'd end up on a forced dose of grimp to regulate her mood. The algae would deaden her senses, make her someone else. Medlevel seemed to prescribe it a lot on this ship.

But Zephyr *did* tend to say the things other people thought but that no one was brave—or

29

stupid—enough to say. But this time, she was wrong. There had to be a good explanation for why the panels were being shipped to Soren.

The fleet wouldn't stay here.

CHAPTER THREE

The tension left Era's body the moment she stepped through the repository doors.

At the far end of the space, rows of tall, silver boxes gleamed from their place behind the glass barrier. The archives took up half the level, and each box contained hundreds of small data storage cubes.

Only the president and board had access to the archival cubes. The data on them was too important, too fragile. But the knowledge would be used to restart civilization once the fleet found New Earth. *Humanity's future.*

Era and Zephyr passed by benches filled with colonists waiting their turn to record messages for loved ones or to view the comms that had arrived for them from other ships.

31

"Fucking glitch," Zephyr said under her breath.

"Shh." Era looked in the direction Zephyr was looking.

Paige, Zephyr's least favorite repository worker, sat at the communications station, handing out holo gear from behind the tall counter. As Era and Zephyr walked past, she wrinkled her nose, smoothed her dark brown hair, and turned away.

"What? She's a glitch." Zephyr sniffed.

Era shook her head.

Paige lived in the same corridor as Zephyr in the singles sector, and according to Zephyr, there was nothing to like about the girl. But whatever had gone down between the two, Zephyr wasn't sharing.

She insisted the reason Paige and the other workers didn't talk to them was because of her father's position, and maybe she was right. The repository workers weren't the first colonists on the *Paragon* to act uncomfortable around them.

Mali, Head Archivist, stood at the archivist station at the back of the room, her eyepiece activated.

Her hands moved in rapid gestures, and

a frown creased her otherwise smooth, brown skin. The streak of gray in her short black hair was the only hint that she was past middle-age.

Era and Zephyr swiped their shift cards across the stationary's scanner, and Mali logged two eyepieces into the system.

"You're late." She handed each of them an eyepiece. "And I've got a bin of handhelds that need fixing."

"When do you not have a bin of handhelds that need fixing?" Zephyr muttered.

"What was that?"

"I'll get the bin," Era said. "We'll get started right away."

Mali shot Zephyr a dour look and offered Era a wide smile. "Thank you, child."

Era and Zephyr skirted the stationary and work tables and headed for the cubics lining the far wall.

"Suck-up," Zephyr said.

"Instigator."

Zephyr rolled her eyes. "I'll meet you in three."

Era fitted her eyepiece against the bridge of her nose and slipped the earbud into place. She continued to the storage cubic and swiped her card along the scanner. Ten months here and Mali had already given her access to storage. No one else on this shift had clearance. Maybe that was another reason the other workers didn't talk to her.

The door slid open, and the lume bar above brightened in response. As she reached for the bin of handhelds, her gaze fell to the small, silver archive cases on the shelf below. Had Mali loaded one with a cube order for the president today?

The president and board had access to all of humanity's collective knowledge...there could be *anything* on those cubes.

She pulled her eyes away from the case. Mali trusted her. She wouldn't mess it up by giving in to her curiosity. But had Mali ever peeked at the data on the archival cubes?

Definitely not. Accessing them without permission would be treason.

Era pulled down the handhelds and grunted under the bin's weight. It'd take four shifts to fix this tech, and by then, there'd be a new bin to start on. Zephyr wasn't wrong about their workload, just stupid to get on Mali's bad side.

Era exited storage and stopped at the sight of the guard at the archivist station.

Tadeo Raines, son of the captain of the *Meso*, spoke with Mali. The *Meso* grew most of the fleet's food, and that made it the second most important ship in the fleet—after the *Paragon*. Which made Tadeo the second most important future-captain.

He, like Zephyr and other senior command level kids, was spending a mandated term aboard the flagship. He served in the guard, directly under the president, but rarely showed up for drops. When he did, he always came with the head guard, Chief Petroff. Never alone.

Zephyr had a bit of a misguided, if understandable, obsession with Tadeo. His natural bronze skin had the kind of glow Era could only hope to get after hours spent under the super helio. He acted like a beacon—the women staring at him from the waiting area proved that. Or maybe they were just wondering if all the rumors about Tadeo were true.

He glanced up, shoving a lock of too-long black hair out of his eyes, and met her gaze. Warmth crept into Era's cheeks, and she walked to cubic three. No way was she telling Zephyr he was here.

Zephyr sat at the table, head in her arms, eyes closed.

"You better pay attention today." Era slid into a chair. "Mali's gonna figure out your skills are worse than basic soon. Don't want to end up plating quin in the galley."

Zephyr groaned and straightened, a scowl on her face. "I can code. I can fix my own handheld. Usually."

"Yeah, you're talking to me right now. Getting a holo to display 'Hello World' doesn't count. Sorry."

"Everyone likes a good welcome message when they activate a handheld. You don't appreciate my skills. And anyway, I'm not the one training for Head Archivist."

Era coughed and adjusted her eyepiece. Mali was approaching the age where she'd choose her successor, but she hadn't said, for sure, that Era was her pick.

Era chose a handheld from the bin and set it down on the table. "Fine. Show me how you fix this."

Zephyr sighed and put her eyepiece on.

Era tapped the handheld to turn it on and twisted her wrist to activate her eyepiece. A three-dimensional infinity symbol twisted in the air in front of them and froze. Zephyr gasped, and her hand flew to her chest.

"What?" Era said.

"I think it's a sign."

"Huh? A sign for what?"

Zephyr slowly lowered her hand to the table and leaned forward. "A sign we're stuck in an infinite loop of pointless drudgery."

Era flared her nostrils, but Zephyr had switched her focus back to the infinity symbol, mock concentration on her face.

Era sighed and gave into the guilt gnawing at her. "Tadeo's out there."

Zephyr sat up straight and deactivated her eyepiece. "And I think I suddenly have a question for Mali."

Era deactivated her own eyepiece and crossed her arms over her chest. "You need to forget about him."

"I didn't judge you when you picked Dritan."

Yes you did. Zephyr's exact words had been "A maintenance sublevel worker? I don't think so. We'll find you someone with a longer life expectancy." Era had ignored the unwelcome advice, but it was the kind best friends give. *A real friend tells you the truth, even when you don't want to hear it.*

She paused, but there was no nice way to say it. "We're like bugs to him, glitches in his shift. He's answered all your attempts at conversation with one word replies."

"Maybe you're a glitch, but I'm—"

"He's twenty and still a half."

"So what?" Zephyr pushed down the sleeve of her suit, revealing the tattoo on her wrist— one half of the infinity symbol. "I'm still a half."

"You're only sixteen. And you're missing my point. He's twenty and still unpaired."

"I know, right? Leaving that kind of genetic potential unpaired should be illegal."

Era sighed. "But...there's something *off* about him. And all the things they say about him—"

"Oooh. All the things." Zephyr opened her mouth and wiggled her fingers in the air. "Where should I start? The one about how some tech died of a broken heart because he wouldn't pair with her? Or maybe the one about how he seduced a sublevel worker, met with her in secret, and then she disappeared. Of course, her body was never recovered—"

Era held her hands up and laughed. "Okay. Stop."

"No. People always talk kak about command level kids. It's nothing new. Who knows what they say about me..." Zephyr squinted at Era.

"Don't look at me. No one's stupid enough to say anything about you to me. But that's irrelevant. Tadeo—have you ever even seen him around with *any* girls?"

Zephyr tilted her head and shrugged. "Maybe he just hasn't found the right girl."

"And you're the right girl."

"Could be."

"Are we sure he's looking for a girl?"

Zephyr's eyes widened. "Yes. We are."

"Okay..."

"Even if he's not, he's still gotta pair with one."

Era shook her head. Population Management allowed pairing with a member of the opposite sex at age sixteen and mandated it by age twenty-one. But that didn't mean everyone preferred the opposite sex. She and Zephyr had been friends with a girl like that back on the *London*. She'd changed a lot after being forced to pair.

39

"Even if he did want to pair with you," Era said, "I *know* he's not gonna give up his claim to the *Meso* to come live on the *London* with you."

"Who says I'm ready to *pair*? I have my implant now, and he's free." Zephyr raised her eyebrows and gave Era a crooked smile. "Not my fault it's perfect timing."

She flipped her long hair over her shoulder, a gleam in her eye. No stopping her when she got that look. She jumped to her feet and hit the button to open the door.

"Zeph—" *Shouldn't have told her.*

The door slid open, revealing Mali on the other side. She had an archive case in one hand and her shift card in the other, poised over the scanner. She blinked at them.

"Era, I need you. I'm doing an urgent records pull for the president. They had a tech in here first shift to update the stationary, and now it's freezing up. Can you take a look?"

Mali's eyes flicked back and forth between them, brows furrowed. "You stay here, Zephyr."

Mali turned to go, and Zephyr pressed her hands together, pleading.

"Can I show her the fix?" Era asked.

"She doesn't have a lot of training on the stationaries."

"Fine," Mali said. "Just get it working."

∞　∞

Era tried to concentrate on the task before her and not the nervous tension emanating from Zephyr as they approached the archivist station.

"I was pulling up records, and the holo blanked. I need to grab this cube order." Mali said, frustration and something *else* edging her voice. She hurried toward the archives.

Era's throat tightened. What kind of records pull was this? And why the urgency?

Zephyr cleared her throat. Tadeo shifted his stance and focused on the far wall behind Era. *Awkward.* He acted like they were invading his personal space whenever he came in here. Definitely something off about him.

Era turned on her eyepiece. The holo had frozen, and a fuzzy white square appeared where the interface should be. A display module issue. The stationary had more power than the handhelds, but they both ran on the same kind of framework. Should be easy to debug.

41

Era pressed two fingers together to access the stationary's display module.

She made a series of gestures, and the blank holo flickered, but nothing changed. The underlying program was still running, then. Why wouldn't the software connect with the display?

Era pulled a handheld diagnostic from under the station and hooked it to the stationary. The bridge interface appeared and displayed the intermediate code.

The program was running an infinite loop.

Era smirked and looked over at Zephyr, but she was busy sneaking glances at Tadeo.

The glitch must have been introduced the last time they updated the system. Era peered at it. *There.* A truncated decimal. How was it that the techs on the *Paragon* always made such simple mistakes?

Either way, it was an easy fix—just a one-line rewrite. She swiped the line of code away, deleting it, and opened the command cloud. She dragged the new commands into the program.

Zephyr cleared her throat. "So, Tadeo. Heard you had some excitement up on level six?"

He nodded but didn't look at her.

Zephyr leaned on the station and narrowed her eyes. "You think the Paragon Guard's competent enough to figure out what really happened? 'Cause I know for sure it had nothing to do with the panels from my father's ship."

Era cringed. Tadeo's face darkened, and he looked at Zephyr. Maybe that was her intention. Sometimes her social filter was as dysfunctional as this tech.

"That's not something I can talk about," Tadeo said, clipping each word short. "Can I get my shift card back now?"

"Yeah," Era said, searching for the card. Mali must have forgotten to return it.

Zephyr got to it first. "They upped your clearance level, huh?" She handed the card to Tadeo and held on to it just a second too long, forcing his hand to brush her own. Tadeo met Zephyr's gaze and held it. His hard expression softened for just a moment, replaced by...something else. Something vulnerable. A *longing*.

Era focused on the stationary and rebooted her eyepiece. Had he looked at her like that before? No. No way she could've missed that.

"I guess they did," Tadeo said, his voice husky.

Zephyr lifted her chin and rubbed her arm. "They're supposed to open up helio sector tomorrow during midbreak. You going?"

What? Zephyr hated the super helio. She said it made her look like Soren incarnated.

Tadeo blinked and hesitated for one long, awkward moment. "Probably."

Oh, no.

"Me, too," Zephyr said. "Maybe we could meet up."

Tadeo glanced toward the glass barrier, his jaw working.

He was going to turn her down. But it'd be for the best. She'd have to move on then, wouldn't she?

Tadeo gave Zephyr a small smile, and a dimple appeared on one cheek. "Yeah. Sure. Let's meet up."

Zephyr's mouth dropped into a little 'o' of surprise, and she darted a look at Era.

Era slammed her mouth shut. *Well, I got that wrong.*

"Great." Zephyr recovered, and she smiled, her face lighting up like a fully charged helio. "I'll see you there."

44

Era reactivated her eyepiece, and the interface loaded this time. Mali was still logged into the system. Her records search ended, and a new file appeared on the interface.

Paragon Sublevel Maintenance Crews: Month 6, Days 08-15: Hull Duty Work Order #284: Level Six: Sector 191.32

Era swallowed hard. Maintenance crew personnel records. This was a work order from months ago, near the time they'd done the hull scans. They were definitely investigating the hull breach. What else could it be?

On the *London*, personnel files were kept for a few months and then purged. Hardly anyone ever reviewed them. And when they did, it was never a good thing.

She should take the eyepiece off. She didn't have the clearance to see this.

After the riots, guards had come to the *London*. Era had been there when her father's replacement had accessed the ship's personnel files. They'd combed through them to find the colonists who'd coordinated the fleet-wide uprising. The traitors had been places on the ship they never should have been, and they'd sent and received comms from others who'd been found guilty.

It had been enough to condemn them. Seven colonists from the *London* were airlocked the following day.

The new file blinked at Era, and she swallowed. Something tugged at her chest, the same sense of *wrongness* that had tried to get her attention earlier, back in the cubic. If Dritan's crew had never had hull duty, hadn't been trained to fix the hull, why would they have been called during a hull breach? To help with the evacuation? There were plenty of guards on level six to handle that...

Mali hadn't left the archives yet, but she'd be done soon.

Era made her decision and tapped the file with one shaking hand. She flicked through the list as fast as she could.

Names. Pictures. Every location each worker had used a shift card during the time period. Dread grew in her gut as she moved through them. She recognized these faces. She'd never spoken to most of them, but she'd seen them all before.

One was a young woman with blue eyes and white-blond hair. *Janet Lanar.* Era had seen her more than a few times up on observation with her little girl. Ja- net had been one of the few people on this ship who'd acted welcoming to Era and Zephyr.

Era rushed through the next few, heart pounding.

His familiar face shimmered into existence before her. He looked so handsome, so confident in his green sublevel suit.

Dritan Corinth.

CHAPTER FOUR

Era's first instinct was to delete Dritan's record, but she stopped herself, her mind racing. Would they blame Dritan and his crew for the breach? Her eyes flicked back and forth between his image and the glass archive doors. Mali walked through them, making the decision for her. There was no time to do anything.

Era's hand shook as she accessed the memory core and deleted her eyepiece signature from the file.

"Did you fix it?" Mali asked, coming around the station, archive case in hand.

Done.

Era exhaled and stepped away from the machine. "Yeah. It works now."

"Good job. Thank you." Mali checked her work and patted Era on the arm. She set the case on the station and opened it.

A row of small silver cubes rested on the spongy inner material. She retrieved the cube with the maintenance crew records from the stationary, added it to the case, and closed it.

Era turned and hurried back to cubic three, her eyes burning. She should have deleted Dritan's records from the cube. But if she had—and they'd discovered it—they'd think she and Dritan were trying to hide something.

Why had Dritan lied to her? In the entire time they'd lived on the *Paragon*, he'd never once mentioned having hull duty. How could he not tell her he'd worked the sector where the breach happened?

Era entered the cubic, sat down at the table, and put her hands over her eyes.

Zephyr walked in after her. "I'm gonna get the best helio burn ever tomorrow. Told you Tadeo just needed the right girl."

Era dragged her hands down her face. She'd just committed a serious crime–and for what? She pressed her lips together and picked up the handheld she and Zephyr had been working on. "We need to finish these."

"There's nothing wrong with Tadeo. I don't know why you—"

"I'm not—come on." Era's voice cracked, and she cleared her throat. "Let's get this done."

Zephyr frowned, but sat down and picked up her eyepiece.

Era activated the handheld, and they stared at the frozen infinity symbol hovering in the air.

"I remember this from the last time you showed me," Zephyr said softly as she gestured and brought up the code.

Era's eyes filled as Zephyr worked. When the riot leaders were airlocked, Zephyr said the president and board were just trying to pin the uprising on someone, make an example of them. Era had brushed off Zephyr's theory.

Those rioters *had* been guilty. The president and board had no choice but to airlock them for the safety of the fleet.

This thing with Dritan, the personnel records—it wasn't like *that*. The president was just doing an investigation into the hull breach. But still. Why had Dritan hidden the truth?

51

Zephyr re-booted the handheld, and the infinity symbol rotated in the air and faded into the mantra of the fleet.

A Better World Awaits.

But will we ever get there?

∞   ∞

Era stepped into the loud din of the galley and followed Zephyr to the mess line. The scent of hot quin grain turned her stomach. She'd thrown it up more times than she could count in the early weeks of her pregnancy. It might never smell good to her again.

She scanned the end of the galley, where the sublevel workers sat. Dritan leaned over a table, hands on the shoulders of two of his crewmates. He broke into a wide grin at something one of them said, and Era's heart grew heavy. Why had he kept the truth from her?

The line moved, and Era took her metal plate and water cup from the galley worker.

"Reduced rations. Again," Zephyr said through gritted teeth.

Era looked down at the small pile of sticky brown quin grain on her plate. A few anemic

52

greens poked out from it. Her stomach flipped.

This was how it had all started a year ago. The riots. The *Meso* had lost some of its crop to the rot, and the shortage seemed to break something in the fleet. Was it happening again?

Era looked back at Zephyr, but her somber expression was gone.

"I'm getting really sick of plain quin, anyway," Zephyr said. "How can the lower levels eat this every single day?

Era shrugged. Command level life on the *London* did have its benefits, not the least of which was a more varied menu. And quin liquor. She and Zephyr had gotten drunk on it while the ship rioted. Era pushed the memory down.

Dritan caught sight of them and pointed to an empty table in their usual spot in the middle of the galley.

Zephyr and Era had tried to sit with his crew once, but the table had fallen silent when they showed up, and a few of his crew members had even shot Zephyr dirty looks. *Never again.* They stuck to the tech tables now.

They walked to the table Dritan had picked for them, and Era dropped down next to him.

Zephyr slid onto the bench across from them and dug her fork into the small pile of grain. "How do they expect us to survive on these rations? The *Meso*'s sure been doing a kak job lately."

Dritan tilted his head to the side and squinted at her. "Yeah, I guess that's what happens when ya send ten sublevel crews down to Soren and only two come back."

Zephyr pursed her lips and folded her hands on the table. "If the *Meso* needs to recruit, they should put out a notice to the other dekas. That's the proper procedure."

Era usually mediated this sort of thing between them, but not today. She kept her eyes on Dritan, stomach churning. How could he lie to her?

"You volunteering to transfer to the *Meso*?" Dritan took a swig of his water. "Then you can let'em know what a kak job they're doing. Or help out. You know how to grow quin, right?"

"I don't see—"

"Nope. You don't."

Zephyr sniffed and shoved a forkful of quin into her mouth.

Dritan exhaled and turned to Era. "So how was your shift?" He leaned in to kiss her but paused an inch from her face. "What's wrong?"

"You lied to me." She kept her voice too low for anyone else to hear.

Dritan glanced toward the sublevel tables, and he took a deep breath.

"The president ordered personnel records," Era said. "How could you not tell me you worked executive sector?"

"I didn't want you to worry, Er."

"I can't believe you never told me you had hull duty..."

"I'm sorry," he said.

"What if...what if they're trying to find someone to blame for the breach?"

"They're not." Dritan bit his lower lip and rubbed Era's leg. "My crew does good work. And they'll see that."

He cleared his throat and turned away to eat. Zephyr was staring at them.

Era pushed her plate toward Zephyr. "You can have mine if you want it."

Zephyr raised her brows, questioning, but Era shook her head and crossed her arms over her chest. Dritan had sounded so sure of himself. Was she overreacting?

The lights in the galley flickered and went out. Conversation died down. Dritan wrapped an arm around Era and drew her close, their argument forgotten. Forgiven.

The scent of boiled quin seemed to intensify. Every murmur, every scrape of a plate, every rustle of a suit seemed louder in the darkness.

"Just another power outage," Dritan murmured. "They'll get it back on soon."

Several minutes passed, and the sirens didn't kick on. She relaxed into Dritan and inhaled his clean scent. The *London* had fewer outages than the *Paragon*, but that was just a perk of being on the deka that manufactured most of fleet's power components.

The lights blinked on, and the entire galley seemed to exhale. Conversation started up again, louder than before.

The shift buzzer sounded, calling an end to last mess and the beginning of night shift.

Dritan kissed Era's neck and held his mouth to her ear. His warm breath sent a pleasant shiver through her body. "It's gonna be okay. You'll see."

"Just don't keep things from me," Era whispered. "Tell me next time."

"I will. I promise."

∞   ∞

The ship is on lockdown.

Sirens. Emergency lights. I race up the deserted stairwell to the first set of doors and swipe my shift card, but the doors won't open.

I rip the panel from the wall. All that's there is a jumble of singed wires, the components around them blackened. But I can fix this. Can't I?

I drop my hands to my waist, seeking my work belt, and my heart drops. My stomach is flat. Empty.

They've aborted my baby.

I choke back a scream and run up the stairs, taking them two at a time. Dritan's on level six. He'll help me. I reach the landing and slip in a pool of dark, viscous liquid.

I crash to the floor. The pool is deep red, sticky, half-dry. The thick metallic scent of it fills my lungs, and bile rises in my throat.

An arc of spattered blood coats the doors and drips down the number six. I try to lift my palms, but they stick to it. "Dritan—"

The door slides open and steals my breath. My body lifts off the landing, and the corridors of level six flash by.

There's a hull breach.

And I'm being sucked into space.

Era's eyes fluttered open in the pitch dark, and she sat up straight, gasping for air, one hand on her still swollen belly.

Just a nightmare. She hadn't had one like that since after her father died.

She reached out a hand and found Dritan's warm body at the edge of the bunk, against the wall.

She cuddled up to him, and he groaned and rolled over in his sleep to wrap her in an embrace. Her body relaxed, and she closed her eyes. Dritan had a way of keeping the nightmares at bay.

CHAPTER FIVE

Era leaned against the sink and stretched her legs. Her hips ached, no matter what she did. She chose a helio sector suit from the rack and set it down on the bench.

Zephyr already had her suit on, and the white fabric made her skin look even paler. "Dritan doesn't like me."

Era sighed and slowly unzipped her suit, trying the whole time to think of a good response. "He does like you. He just takes a while to get to know."

"Funny, he seemed to get to know you pretty fast."

"It's just—sometimes you say things."

"What?" Zephyr placed her hands on her hips. "The things I say never bothered you before."

"They don't bother me..."

"Ha. Told you he doesn't like me." Zephyr faced the mirror and ran her fingers through her hair, working out tangles.

Era frowned and tucked her short brown hair behind her ears. Much more practical. So maybe Zeph wasn't Dritan's favorite person in the fleet. But he knew Era cared for her, and that was enough for him.

Era finished removing her boots and suit and placed them in a locker. She was stepping into the helio suit when a young woman left the showers. The woman scowled at Era's bare belly.

Era's cheeks warmed, and she zipped up the suit. Not like it covered anything. It was sleeveless, ended mid-thigh, and hugged her curves, accentuating her growing bump in a way her regular suits didn't.

She walked to the sink and tapped it to rinse her hands in the small trickle of water that came out. Then she grabbed a rag from the bin of suit scraps and dried her hands.

"You ever gonna tell me what the big

deal was last night at mess?" Zephyr asked.

"If I do, it won't be here." Era eyed the woman again in the mirror. The woman caught Era looking, frowned, and turned away to finish dressing.

Zephyr adjusted her too-tight suit and struck a pose in front of the mirror. She danced around Era to get to the door. "Can't keep my lover waiting. Wouldn't wanna ruin his whole midbreak."

Era rolled her eyes and followed.

Dritan had eased her mind about the hull breach investigation last night, but she'd still half-expected guards to storm the cubic and arrest him. She'd been wrong, though. Only her nightmare had interrupted her sleep.

Era and Zephyr turned the corner and hit the wave of heat emanating from helio sector's open doorway. The tension fled Era's body, and her skin tingled in response to the warmth. She picked up her pace. Unlike the burn Zephyr would get, the super helio would give Era's skin a warm glow and energize her. It always did. If only they opened helio sector for recreation every day.

A guard, his face coated in sweat, stood next to the scanner. He nodded to them as they swiped their shift cards.

They stepped into the vast space, and Era took a deep breath, relishing the sweet air. A new Earth would smell like this, infused with the clean air plants make.

The super helio hovered near the high ceiling, too bright to look at, and a crowd of colonists basked beneath it.

Helio sector's tall, white hydropods had been moved to the edges of the space. The *Paragon* had hundreds of them—more than Era had ever seen in one place. Probably nowhere near the number the *Meso* had, but still more than any of the other dekas. And this wasn't even all of them. There were more hydropods on Zero Deck. Other sectors that were off-limits—where they grew and made medicine.

Greens poked out of each pod, creating an effect like the trees Zephyr had images of on her family's cubes. Tough to believe these lush greens were the same wilted fare turned out by the galley cooks.

A few colonists strolled the edge of the massive space, and Era and Zephyr

62

dropped in behind them.

Zephyr gripped Era's hand. "He's here."

Tadeo sat near some pods ahead, alone, his arms crossed over his knees, staring out at the crowd gathered in the center of the room. His straight black hair had fallen into his eyes, but he seemed oblivious to it.

"Well, go talk to him," Era said.

"Come with me," Zephyr said, dragging Era toward Tadeo.

He glanced up as they approached, and Zephyr dropped Era's hand. His gaze went straight to Zephyr, and his brown eyes brightened.

"Why you sitting by yourself?" Zephyr asked. "Everyone's over there."

"I'm not here to see everyone."

Zephyr looked like she was about to swoon right into Tadeo's waiting lap.

Someone really needed to file an image of this boy's face in the archives, under the word 'enigma'. "I'm going to go wait for Dritan."

Zephyr nodded without looking at Era and dropped down next to Tadeo on the floor.

Era continued walking the space and kept her eye on the entrance.

She'd walked half the sector when she saw the guards up ahead. Her stomach clenched, and she slowed her pace.

The guard closest to her stood straight, sweat dripping down his face, and watched the crowd. One hand rested on his pulse gun, as if he thought he might actually need to use it here.

Behind the guards, President Nyssa Sorenson and her fourteen-year-old daughter Tesmee sat on a blanket. Instead of standard helio suits, they wore sleeveless beige suits that looked new.

Era let out a breath and tried not to stare as she walked past, but she couldn't help herself. She'd been here months and had only caught a few glimpses of the president and Tesmee.

The president wore her hair styled in a perfect blond bun kept in place by shiny metal pins. But her well-groomed appearance was marred by the deep lines creasing her face and the dark circles under her eyes. She shifted on the blanket and glanced toward the exit.

Tesmee looked nothing like her mother. Era had seen Tesmee's father once. He'd been of Earth-Asian ancestry. Tesmee had his eyes and his straight black hair. She stared out at the

64

crowd, shoulders slumped, longing on her face.

Tesmee's father had died in a transport accident when the fleet first got to Soren two years ago. If rumor in the fleet was to be believed, she wasn't ever allowed to leave Command home level by herself.

Era tore her gaze from the girl and headed for the crowd at the center. Dritan should be here. Zephyr and Tadeo were still in the same spot she'd left them. They talked, sitting close enough to touch, but neither of them looked at the other.

Era settled on the hard tile floor, and a moment later Dritan plopped down beside her. He pressed his lips to hers for a quick kiss, then cocked his head in Zephyr's direction. "Went after the heir of the *Meso*, huh? Guess heading up one ship isn't enough."

Era jabbed him in the side. "Stop it. Give her a chance. She's easy to love once you get to know her."

"I didn't say I didn't like her."

"Well she thinks you don't." Era lowered her voice. "Any news on the breach?"

"They're looking into the panels we did." Dritan rubbed his arm. "But they'll see our work was good. Are you feeling okay today?"

"Haven't been sick at all." Era leaned back on her elbows. If Dritan wasn't worried, why should she be? The president would see his work was good, and this would all go away.

A young girl with dark skin and braids bounced past, laughing as another child chased her. Era smiled. Today would feel special for them, a day free of the boredom and routine of hours spent in caretaker sector. Would she and Dritan someday sit here like this, watching their own child play?

Dritan must have had a similar thought because he gently placed a hand over the rise of her belly. A tiny flutter reverberated through Era's womb, and she gasped.

"What?" Dritan sat up straight.

"Nothing. I thought I felt..." It was too soon for that, wasn't it? *Babies* moved. A "collection of cells" didn't.

"You thought you felt what?"

"I thought..." *Another* tiny flutter. Era licked her lips and glanced sidelong at the couple sitting next to them.

"I think I just felt it move," she whispered.

Dritan looked at her stomach. When he met her gaze, his hazel eyes had a new shine to them. "You sure? Does it mean..."

Does it mean our baby's healthy?

"I'm not—" Era clamped her mouth shut, her eyes drawn to a scene at the entrance.

A group of guards had walked through the doors. The one at the front, with silver-brown hair and broad shoulders, turned and lifted his comcuff to his mouth. Chief Petroff.

Era leaned into Dritan, every muscle in her body tight.

The chief gestured to the other guards. They activated their eyepieces and began moving through the crowd.

The president and Tesmee came into view at the far side of the room, accompanied by two of their guards. They were heading for the exit. Era clutched Dritan's arm and felt him wince as her nails dug into him.

One of the guards stopped in front of a group of colonists near Era and Dritan. A man rose to his feet, and Dritan tensed beneath Era's tight grip.

The man was one of Dritan's crew members—one of the maintenance workers from the list. He lunged for the guard and ripped the pulse gun from his holster. Then he darted forward, pushed through the colonists blocking his path, and went straight for Tesmee and the president.

The guards didn't see him coming. He ducked around them and tackled Tesmee to the floor.

The area around Era grew quiet as the colonists near Era saw what she saw. The man had the pulse gun pressed against Tesmee's temple. Her eyes were wide, riveted to her mother. The president stood still, her face pale.

Dritan leapt to his feet. Era tried to drag him back down, but he brushed her off and jogged straight for the guards. A small moan escaped Era's lips, and she went after him. What did he think he could do that the guards couldn't?

Dritan stopped just behind the uncertain guards, his body rigid, his fists clenched tight at his sides. Era reached him and laid a hand on his arm.

The attacker's face was coated in sweat, and the hand holding the pulse gun to Tesmee's temple shook. His wild eyes were focused on the President. "...I will. Gonna kill her.

You think I care what happens to me? You took everything from me."

"Stop. Let her go." The president's voice wavered. "We'll forget about this. You're clearly—"

"The Defect is a lie. A lie. You killed our baby. You killed my wife—sent her to that planet. You're gonna pay for that."

The president went white and shook her head. She stole a glance at her guards, but none of them seemed to know what to do.

The Defect is a lie?

Dritan shifted, and Era squeezed his arm. He pulled away from her and stepped in front of the guards.

"Wait." The president jerked one hand out to stop the guards. To stop Dritan.

But he walked past her and squatted down a few feet in front of his crewmate. "Sam."

"Dritan." Recognition dawned on Sam's face. "Your wife—your wife's pregnant. Dritan, it's a lie. The Defect isn't real. They'll kill yours like they killed mine. I gotta stop her. One by one, everyone dies—"

"Sam. Listen to me. You said Lynn was proud to serve on Soren. That she believed in this fleet."

Tears began to leak from Sam's eyes, and he looked back at the president. "She killed them." His nostrils flared, and he pressed the pulse gun deeper into Tesmee's temple. She whimpered.

The president lifted a hand to her mouth. The rest of the guards arrived, finally aware of what was taking place. They clustered near the president, pulse guns primed.

Dritan inched closer. "Sam, look at me. Lynn would never want you to take another kid's life."

"It doesn't matter now. Nothing matters. They're gonna take me out, too, and she's coming with me." Sam shifted his hate-filled gaze to the president, and adjusted his finger on the pulse gun. One small movement, and it would go off, taking a chunk of Tesmee's skull with it.

Dritan held out a hand and said something too low for anyone but Tesmee and Sam to hear. Sam hesitated and stared at the high ceiling for a long moment.

His whole body went limp, and he shoved the pulse gun into Dritan's waiting palm. The guards were on Sam in seconds, and Tesmee scrambled into her mother's arms.

Dritan handed the pulse gun to a guard and strode to Era. He wrapped his arms around her. She buried her face in his chest and inhaled, tears pricking her eyes.

She hit his chest. "Stupid. What if he pulsed you?"

Dritan brushed a short strand of hair out of Era's face. "But he didn't. He was going to kill her. You saw that."

He stiffened, looking over Era's head. She turned to find President Sorenson, Tesmee, and Chief Petroff standing before her. The chief activated his eyepiece and began to gesture commands.

The president gave Dritan a tight nod. "Thank you."

"Sam's coming down hard off grimp. He never would have—"

The president's face darkened, and she held up a hand, "We will take care of it from here. Thank you for your help."

"President Sorenson." Chief Petroff pointed at Dritan. "This man's on the list."

The president's eyes narrowed, and she turned and grabbed Tesmee by the arm. When she looked back at the chief, her expression was blank, unreadable. "Take him in."

71

CHAPTER SIX

Era's stomach knotted, and she pressed against Dritan.

Chief Petroff dropped his hand to his pulse gun at his waist. "You need to come with us."

Dritan placed his hand against the small of Era's back. "It'll be okay."

The feeling seeped from her limbs as he stepped in front of her and followed Chief Petroff to the exit. A group of guards filed past, several colonists in tow. All of them members of Dritan's crew.

Tadeo crossed in front of Era and approached one of the guards. Era turned to find Zephyr at her side.

"What happened?"

"They arrested Dritan." Era choked on the words. "They're gonna blame him for the hull breach."

Zephyr's eyes widened, and she laid her hands on Era's shoulders. "You gotta calm down. Breathe."

I can't. "He saved Tesmee—"

"Shh. Come on." Zephyr grabbed Era by the arm and pulled her toward the exit.

Era took deep breaths, trying to calm the panic rising within her as Zephyr led her down the corridor. They reached the deserted dressing area, and Zephyr pushed her down onto the cold metal bench.

She checked the stalls and came back. Every inch of her exposed skin had taken on a scarlet hue that contrasted sharply with the white of her suit. "Now, what happened?"

"You're burnt," Era said tonelessly. *They arrested him. There's nothing I can do.* Era put her head in her hands and willed her heart to slow down.

"Where is Dritan?"

"One of his crew members was coming off grimp and attacked Tesmee. Dritan stopped him. They took them both away."

"Whoa. That's—but why would they arrest

him? I don't understand. You said he helped Tesmee?"

"He saved her."

"Are you sure they arrested him?"

"Yes. Maybe." *I don't know.*

"If he saved Tesmee..."

Era lifted her head and swallowed. "I did something I shouldn't have when I fixed the stationary yesterday. The president's file pull was ready, and I looked at it. She requested personnel records from months ago, back when maintenance installed new panels where the breach happened. Dritan's crew was the one that installed them."

Zephyr sucked in a breath and sank down on the bench beside her.

"They'll pin the breach on them," Era said. "Make examples out of them, just like you said they did with the riot leaders they airlocked."

"No. I never should've said that kak. Those rioters were guilty. You know they were."

"But Dritan worked on that sector. And a member of his crew just-just attacked the president's daughter."

"And Dritan protected her," Zephyr said. "He's never even been in the brig for so much as a fist fight."

75

Era shook her head and blinked back tears.

"They're just questioning him." Zephyr squeezed Era's shoulder. "You'll see. He'll be out of there by last mess."

"I never should have looked at those files," Era whispered.

The shift buzzer sounded, announcing the end of midbreak.

Zephyr stood up. "Get dressed. You're gonna go and do your job like the loyal fleet colonist you are."

"Loyal? But I looked—"

The door slid open, and a group of women walked in.

"Anyone would have looked." Zephyr kept her voice low. "You and Dritan follow the rules. You don't complain. You never get in trouble...the president wishes we were all like you. Now come on."

The pressure in Era's chest lightened at Zephyr's words, but not by much. She stood, took her black tech suit from the locker, and stripped off the helio suit.

Dritan was a good worker. He'd never been in trouble. And he *did* just save Tesmee. Zephyr had to be right. They were just questioning him.

76

Era stepped into her suit and gently zipped it up. Dritan would be waiting for her at last mess. Now all she had to do was get through the next six hours.

∞　∞

Six hours never felt so long.

Era sat in a recording cubic across from the colonist. "Where's this going?"

"The *Seattle*," he said.

Era slid a blank cube into her handheld and activated her eyepiece. The colonist couldn't see it, but her eyepiece displayed a holo interface between the two black vidrelay rods on the table. She tapped the interface and nodded to the colonist to begin.

"Name: Orin Xian. Message for: Hani Xian. Destination: *Seattle*," he said.

Era tried to focus on his message, tried to pay attention to ensure he didn't say anything on the flagged list—nothing about the riots, or the president, or anything negative about the *Paragon* and the fleet.

But the scene from helio sector played itself over and over in her mind. Sam pressing the pulse gun to Tesmee's head, Tesmee's wide eyes, Dritan inching closer.

The Defect is a lie.

Before everything on Earth had gone wrong, they'd been in the golden age of genetic modification—the science to solve all the world's problems. Only it hadn't. It'd made everything worse. That gen-mod technology caused a worldwide famine that led to the Last War. Not many were protected from the fallout.

But before that, they'd tried to improve human immunity. It had worked, but they discovered, too late, that it affected the children of those who had been modified. So many children died from the Defect. Their organs didn't develop right. They only lived for minutes or days after being born.

After the wars, Infinitek Group had stepped in and provided a way to save humanity from extinction. A lucky few had made it onto their fleet, but all carried the altered genes. The Legacy Code.

The Legacy Code was the mistake that followed them after Earth. A known fact. It *couldn't* be a lie.

The man stopped speaking, and Era

tapped the vidrelay interface to end the recording. She popped the cube from her handheld and pushed to her feet.

"Thank you," the man said.

She nodded and followed him to the door.

The waiting area was empty. Era brought the cube to the table where Paige sat managing the comm cases. One of the new transfers, a narrow-faced girl with dull brown hair, sat beside her.

"This is going to the *Seattle*," Era said.

Paige leaned back in her chair. "And?"

"And your job is to collect the cubes, so here's this one."

"But you're so very good at doing everyone's job. Wouldn't you like to learn this one next?"

The new transfer's hand flew to her mouth, and she tittered.

Era flushed and rotated the outgoing case. Great. Paige had a sidekick now. Like she needed to deal with two of them.

Binary glitches. She unlatched it, found the container labeled *Seattle*, and dropped the cube in.

Mali walked up to the table. "Is there a reason Era's sorting comms?"

Paige gave Mali a sweet smile. "Just showing her how it works."

"You were instructed to train *Helice* today. I'll have the outgoing comms now. The guard'll be by soon to pick them up."

"They're ready to go." Paige stood up and latched the case shut. She handed it to Mali and avoided making eye contact with Era.

"Era, I need to talk to you before you leave," Mali said. "Come with me, please."

Paige pursed her lips, and her face turned a nice shade of wilted-galley-green. *Serves her right.* Era threw her shoulders back and followed Mali.

She led her to the end of the repository, to a table beside the tall glass wall that shielded the archives. The history of the Defect was in there. The colonists who restarted civilization would have the resources and time to find a cure.

But right now, only the president and board had access to those files. Not a grimp addict who worked the sublevels. Era shook her head. Sam didn't know anything about the Defect. How could he?

"Have a seat." Mali sat at the table and laid the comm case next to her. Era slid into one of the chairs and placed her palms flat on the cold metal table.

She doesn't seem upset with me, but why the private talk?

Mali folded her hands together and regarded Era for a moment. "I need to start training my replacement soon. I want that person to be you."

Era's eyes widened. "I—thank you."

"So is this something you'd like to do? Being Head Archivist is a big responsibility. The *Paragon* will be your home for the rest of your life."

Era looked down at her hands. Before the last few days, she'd have said yes in a heartbeat. But now? Did she want to stay here? It was the safest ship in the fleet...wasn't it? Dritan had talked about making a home on the *Paragon*, finding a way to remain on board when their five-year placement terms were up. An archivist position would guarantee they'd be allowed to stay.

The shift buzzer sounded, and Era glanced behind her. The other workers began to exit the level, and Zephyr waited for her by the door.

"Why me?"

Mali's brow furrowed. "You're young, yet responsible, and you're a hard worker. Your father taught you better than most of the techs on this ship. I think you have a natural affinity for this type of work."

Era nodded and looked toward the doors again, torn between Mali's offer and her desire to run to last mess and find Dritan. But she needed to give Mali an answer.

Era's father would've been so proud if he knew she'd been offered a position as archivist. And didn't she love this place? The silver boxes beckoned to her from their sanctuary beyond the barrier. This job really meant something. And Dritan...he liked it here. Had the guards let him go yet?

"If you're not sure..."

"No, it's just..." Had Mali heard yet? What would she think if she knew Dritan was wrapped up in something awful? Era licked her lips. "In helio sector, during midbreak, a colonist attacked the president's daughter."

Mali's eyes widened. "You saw this?"

"My husband knew the man from shift and stopped him from hurting her. They arrested the traitor and took my husband in...for questioning." Era's eyes burned, and Mali reached out to touch her hand.

"The president will be grateful for what your husband did."

Era dropped her hands into her lap. "I want to. I do want to be an archivist."

Mali nodded. "I'd hoped you'd say yes. I had to get approval before I could ask you. We'll start training you on the system tomorrow." She narrowed her eyes, and Era turned to see Zephyr hurrying toward them, her face still flushed from its exposure to the super helio.

"Everyone on free shift's been called to observation," Zephyr said. "We need to go. Now."

Era's stomach dropped, and she gripped the table.

"Do you know why?" Mali asked.

"They're airlocking a traitor."

CHAPTER SEVEN

Era and Zephyr joined the crowd in the stairwell. The handrail felt insubstantial beneath Era's hand, and the bodies around her passed in and out of the edges of her blurred vision as they made the slow climb to observation. It was all so surreal. *Holo*.

If only she could gesture, make the scene disappear, return her to a reality where Dritan hadn't been taken by the guard, and a member of his crew wasn't about to be airlocked.

Era had shut herself in her cubic the day they airlocked the traitors on the *London*. She couldn't watch it again, not after what she saw the day of the riots.

They'd been docked at Soren for one year when the riots happened. The captain, the

85

crew, and all of their family members blockaded themselves on the bridge to wait it out. Dritan had been working when it started, and Zephyr had to stop Era from going to find him.

She and Zephyr huddled in a corner, sipping quin liquor and listening as the reports came in. Three ships had gone dark, including the *Kyoto*, which had been docked right next to them.

The *Kyoto* had been dark an hour when the rioters there airlocked the captain and his crew. One of the bloated corpses drifted so close to the bridge of the *London* that it slammed into the glass and stayed there, staring at them through bloodshot eyes. Sightless. Empty.

The president ended the riots by sending guards to each of the dekas. In less than a shift, the guards took back the *Kyoto* and airlocked the traitors.

That was the day Era knew she couldn't live so many levels above Dritan anymore—knew he was the half to complete her infinity.

They reached observation. The doors were open, and no one bothered to swipe their shift cards. Era froze at the threshold, her gaze riveted to Soren's blood-red surface.

Someone cursed behind her, and Zephyr dragged Era onto the deck. The incoming crowd pushed them forward until they reached the front.

At least two dozen guards had lined up across the glass expanse, their pulse guns out and primed. Chief Petroff and Tadeo flanked the president. She stood tall, the tendons in her neck taut, as her unblinking gaze swept over the gathering colonists.

The board members were arrayed beside the chief. Four men. One woman. They represented the ten manufacturing dekas, in theory, yet each of them had lived on the flagship for their entire lives.

Chief Petroff lifted an amplifier, a black box smaller than a handheld, to his mouth. He cleared his throat, and the sound traveled through the room.

Tadeo stepped closer to the president, his jaw working, and adjusted his pulse gun in his grip.

"Silence on the deck," the chief said.

The murmuring died down, and the president took the amplifier and lifted it to her mouth. She scanned the row of vigilant guards beside her and lifted her chin. "At the end of first shift yesterday, level six experienced a hull breach. We have completed our investigation. What happened yesterday was no accident. It was sabotage."

Gasps echoed through the crowd.

President Sorenson backed up a step and switched the amplifier to her other hand. "Three maintenance crew workers have confessed to sabotaging this ship. Several of our guards were injured. Many lives could have been lost. This was their intention."

Three. Sam. And who else?

Era's legs weakened beneath her, and she raised a hand to her chest. Zephyr looped an arm around her back, lending support.

The president paused, waiting for the noise to die down. "If we ever want to find our better world, each of us must continue to do our duty to the fleet. There may be more traitors lurking among us. We are instituting a strict curfew. All colonists must be in their assigned cubics during night shift, unless I personally grant you an exemption for critical ship work. If you witness any suspicious behavior, you must report it immediately. If anyone is found to be hiding or with- holding information about such occurrences, they will be held accountable."

Dritan didn't do anything. He wasn't a traitor. No mention of the attack on Tesmee. The guards didn't save her. Dritan did.

Chief Petroff took the amplifier from the president's trembling grip. She clasped her hands together over her abdomen and said something to the chief.

He spoke into his comcuff, activated his eyepiece, and held the amplifier to his mouth.

"The penalty for treason against the fleet is death." The chief stood straighter. "The following colonists have been found guilty of treason—"

The crowd erupted, and hands raised in the air. Era's gaze traveled along an invisible line from pointing fingers to a location beyond the glass. She pressed her fist hard into her chest.

They'd already airlocked the traitors.

Three objects drifted through the bright stream of light that originated from outside the main airlock. Two pale objects, a third, darker—all of them too far away to see in any detail. Then they were gone, beyond the reach of the lights.

Unbearable pressure expanded in Era's chest, and tears sprung into her eyes.

"Samuel Smith, *Meso* transfer, planned the attacks. His co-conspirators were Tatiana Carizo and Jonas Keen, also of the *Meso*."

Tears flooded Era's vision, blurring the scene. Not Dritan.

Zephyr pulled on Era's arm, and they joined the subdued crowd moving toward the exit.

"I told you Dritan would be okay," Zephyr whispered.

"Come to my level with me?"

"I will."

∞   ∞

Dritan was pacing the entrance to their cubic when Era and Zephyr arrived. The heavy pressure in Era's rib cage dissolved, and her limbs turned the consistency of tech adhesive gel. She rushed to him, shaky with relief, and he drew her close.

Era held a hand up to Zephyr. "Thanks."

"I'm sorry about those...about your crew members," Zephyr said.

Dritan didn't answer, and after a long pause, Zephyr turned and left.

"When they said three..." Era tightened her grip on Dritan, willing the shaking to subside.

"You should go to mess. You need to eat." Dritan's voice was gruff, pained.

How could she eat after what had just happened? She needed sleep. It would take this all away. She shook her head, and Dritan swiped his card across the scanner. Era followed him into their cubic.

He activated their helio and began to unlace his boots. He gave up before he had them off and sat down hard on the bunk, hands clenched on his thighs. Era sat next to him, but he didn't look at her. She took off her boots, dropped them to the floor, and rested a gentle hand on his arm. "If you don't want to talk about it right now..."

"From the questions they asked, I think they found sabotaged panels. I think—the rivets were purposely damaged before they were installed. I'd never install a rivet that looked like that." Dritan's voice cracked. "Tati and Jonas covered for Sam while he did it. I never thought..."

Era laid a hand on his shoulder. "You couldn't have known."

"No. I should've," he said. "The way the three of them talked...I could've stopped them."

"How did they talk?"

Dritan shrugged off her hand and crossed to the wall. He slumped against it and stared down at the crumbling black rubber tiles. "They'd all lost people on Soren. Said the kind of kak lots of people say."

"Like what?"

"They called the traitors from the riots martyrs, said they died for 'the cause.'"

"Martyrs?"

Dritan chewed his lower lip and didn't answer.

"They risked all of our lives, just to get to the president." Era hugged her knees to her chest. She hesitated, then asked the question that had been lurking at the back of her mind since helio sector. "Dritan...what'd you say to Sam to get him to give you that pulse gun?"

"I knew he was ready to kill Tesmee. So I told him what I thought he needed to hear."

"And what was that?"

Dritan took a deep breath. "I asked him if he wanted to be remembered as a martyr. Or a murderer."

Era exhaled and leaned against the

wall. Sublevel workers calling traitors martyrs? She'd never even heard of this. It was the kind of talk that could get someone airlocked. That *had*.

What else did his crew members say that Dritan hadn't shared? Did he say these things, too? Era opened her mouth to ask, but Dritan held up a hand.

"My crew. Or, what's left of my crew," he said. "We got transfer orders today."

Era's pulse quickened at the anguish in his voice.

"They're sending us down to Soren."

CHAPTER EIGHT

oren.

The word sucked the air from the cubic, left Era struggling to breathe.

"It's only one solar cycle," Dritan said.

Era placed a hand over her stomach. "This is a mistake. The *Paragon*'s exempt from the draft."

"Not anymore," he said. "They're sending three crews down."

"When?"

"I have to be at the hangar bay tomorrow. First shift."

Less than nine hours. "You can't go. I'll talk to Zephyr, have her—"

"No," he said. "It wasn't right for us to be exempt in the first place."

"They're just doing this to punish you for what those traitors did."

"The workers on the *London* did their duty. It's my turn."

Something broke inside Era, and she jumped off the bunk, tears brimming in her eyes. Her lower abdomen ached in response to her quick movement, and she gritted her teeth. "By 'workers,' you mean sublevel workers. You think the president would ever send Tesmee down there? You mean nothing to them. You're expendable, just a body to use up in the mines. I'm starting to understand why Sam felt like he needed to do what he did."

"Dammit, Era. Don't say that kak."

"Zephyr said they're not even working on the jumpgate anymore. She thinks they're expanding the subcity. That we're never leaving here." Era lowered her voice. "I didn't believe her."

Dritan crossed his arms and gave a slight shake of his head.

Era picked up her boots and hurled them at the door. "Fuck." They hit with a loud thunk and dropped to the tiles.

She sank to the floor and held her hand to her mouth. Hot tears spilled down her cheeks, and she tasted their salty warmth on her lips.

Dritan knelt in front of her, placing his hands on her shoulders. "I'm going to come back to you."

Era sniffed. "I bet everyone says that."

"But I mean it. I will come back. I'm doing my job, and I'll be here with you when..." he placed his hand over the curve of her belly. "I promise. I'm coming back."

Era stared into his hazel eyes and forced her jaw to loosen. "How can you promise something like that? Did your parents tell you that, too, before they went out on hull duty?"

Dritan recoiled from her, his face creased with pain.

Era placed her hands on either side of her and dug her fingernails into the spongy, gritty surface of the rubber tiles. "I'm sorry," she whispered.

Dritan got to his feet and returned to the bunk. He sat there, shoulders hunched, and stared straight ahead. "You knew my job when you decided to pair with me. I'll never be a tech or a member of the guard. This is what I was born into—what I've been trained to do."

Era had promised herself she'd never shame him, and now she had. She stumbled to her feet and went to him. "I'm sorry. I shouldn't have said that. I just...I'm scared. But you're right. You'll come back. Of course you will."

When Dritan looked at her, his eyes had tears in them. He took her by the arms and pulled her onto the bunk.

They laid together, the pain between them a living thing, pulsing in the silence. He stroked her hair, and she pressed her ear to the coarse fabric of his suit, listening to the reassuring thump of his heart.

A dull ache throbbed in her chest, a certainty that nothing would ever be right again. If she could do it over, make different choices, she never would've asked Zephyr to get them a term here. Things had been simpler on the London. Maybe if they were still there, Zephyr's father could have kept Dritan from the draft.

"Era." Dritan's fingers stilled, and he stopped running them through her hair. "Don't talk about the president, the board— any of it. Please. Just keep your head down and wait for me."

Era wiped the tears from her cheeks and

didn't answer. What could she say? *I'll die if I lose you.*

"It'll go fast," he said. "I'll be back before you—if you..."

Before I have the baby. If I have the baby. The thought of what would happen if the baby had the Defect hung in the air between them, unspoken.

"I'm sorry I have to leave you like this." He placed a hand on Era's stomach. "I wanted to be here."

"I don't want to stay up here without you," Era said, crying again. "There has to be a way to get you out of this."

"I have to do my part. Just one solar cycle." His voice was firm.

One solar cycle. 150 days. 150 chances for something to go very wrong on Soren.

Dritan gently rolled Era off his chest and held himself above her, meeting her eyes. "I will come back to you. And I'll think about you every second I'm not with you."

Era's pulse quickened, and she pulled him close, crushing her lips to his. The pain in her throat eased. He kissed her again, slowly this time, and ran his hand down her body, stopping to cup her breast under her suit. Her nipples hardened against the rough fabric, and she let out a small moan.

A shiver curled down her spine as he brought his lips to her ear and nibbled there. He teased a trail along her jawline with the tip of his tongue, bringing his mouth back to hers.

Era trembled and pressed a hand against his chest. "I need you now."

He stood, pulled off his boots, and unzipped his suit in one swift movement, never taking his eyes off hers. A sheen of sweat coated his lean muscles. He shrugged his suit the rest of the way off. He was ready for her.

She sat up and yanked on the zipper of her own suit. It stuck, then ripped away, the worn fabric finally giving up.

Dritan pulled her to her feet, and her suit fell into a crumpled heap of ruin on the floor. She stepped out of it and placed her hand against his chest. Faint scars he'd gotten in the sublevels criss-crossed his body, and she traced one of them down his abdomen, her fingertips tingling. He lifted her wrist to his mouth to kiss the infinity tattoo that matched the one on his own wrist.

He crushed his lips to hers and

nudged her toward the bunk, hungry for the same release she needed. They fell into it, and she closed her eyes, relishing the feel of his warm body pressed against her, the feel of his tongue as it found her own.

He'd fill her up, make her feel whole, safe, wanted. She'd savor this night. It could be the last they ever had together.

∞   ∞

Era sat on their bunk, watching as Dritan stuffed his spare uniform into his bag. Her eyes drifted to the now nearly empty shelf. Only one thing remained. A small folded scrap of exec-standard bedding.

"Mali picked me as her replacement for archivist." Era forced out the words. "I said yes."

Dritan hefted his bag and tossed it across his body. He gave her a small, proud smile. "I knew she would."

He went to the door, but when he hit the button, the door didn't budge.

"Come here. Watch," Dritan said. "You need to learn how to fix this now."

Era reluctantly got up and went to the door.

101

He slipped a panel off the wall, pulled out a bundle of wires, and twisted the ends of a few, pointing to each one as he did it.

"If these don't connect, it won't open."

Era stared hard at the wires. *Don't work. Lock us inside. Make Dritan miss his transport.*

He inserted the twisted wires back in their spot and hit the button. The door opened.

"Got it now?"

The lump in Era's throat expanded, and she nodded. Dritan tilted his head to the side, and with a sad smile, he offered his hand. She took it, and he led her into the corridor.

The pit in Era's stomach grew as each step brought them closer to the hangar bay. She tightened her grip on Dritan's hand, memorized the feel of his warm touch, the way his larger hand encompassed her small one, how each long finger felt intertwined with her own.

The climb down to zero deck brought back visions of her nightmare. She'd had it again, had lain awake afterward. Dritan wouldn't be here to keep the nightmares away any longer.

No matter how she wished this wasn't happening, how she wished she could freeze time and keep him, the bay drew ever closer. And then they were there.

A guard stood outside the doors holding a scanner. Dritan lifted his shift card, and the guard logged it.

Dritan gave it to Era. "Keep it safe. I'll need it when I get back."

She nodded mutely and shoved his card in her pocket.

Acrid fumes burned her throat as they stepped into the dim hangar bay. A dozen battered transports were docked here, small and pathetic in a vast space that had been built to hold so many more.

Her nails bit into her palms, and she forced herself to unclench her fists. Stupid to hate machines that were just doing their job. The president and board were the ones sending Dritan down to Soren.

A crowd of colonists and their loved ones gathered at the loading area—tense, waiting. Era recognized most of them from the galley and the personnel files she'd seen at the repository.

As Era and Dritan reached them, a child cried out from somewhere in the crowd. Era's heart lurched, and she turned toward the source of the sound. The blonde, Janet Lanar, snuggled close to her husband, their small daughter in her arms.

Lucky enough to have a healthy child, then ripped away from her family by the draft. None of this was fair.

Era tore her gaze from the little girl's face and gripped Dritan's hand tighter. He squeezed three times. She blinked away tears and squeezed back. *I. Love. You.*

Dritan's mother had taught him that. It was one of the only things he remembered about her. Would he get the chance to hold their child's hand—show his love without needing a word?

They stood in silence and waited for the transport pilot to begin the boarding process. Her palm grew slick against Dritan's, but she didn't let go.

Zephyr hurried through the doors. She rushed over to them, her face red, hand pressed to her side. "I heard at mess. If I had more time, I could've sent a comm to my father, or—"

"I wouldn't have let you." Dritan narrowed his eyes and shook his head. "I won't stay here while my crew risks their lives."

An alarm blared from the transport,

and its heavy metal door began its slow descent to the ground. Era's stomach dropped. Dritan lifted her chin and turned her face away from the transport.

Breathe. This was it. He'd be gone soon. She needed to remember. She burned his image into her mind. The curves of his face, smooth dark skin, high cheekbones, hazel eyes glistening with tears that matched her own. And that way he looked at her that let her know how much she was loved.

"I'm coming back," he whispered.

Era nodded. She'd break down in front of everyone if she tried to speak.

The pilot began calling out the list of names. Janet and her family, engaged in a tearful good-bye, stepped into Era's line of sight.

No. This was happening too fast. She couldn't let Dritan leave. She had to find a way to keep him here.

"Dritan Corinth," the pilot called out.

Era's body went cold, and the pressure in her chest made it hard to breathe. Dritan wrapped his strong arms around her and pressed his lips to hers. Would this be the last time she kissed him?

The embrace ended too soon.

"I love you." His eyes shone.

"I love you." Era barely heard her voice.

Dritan's eyes flicked to her belly, and he rested his hand there for a moment before stepping away. He looked at Zephyr. "You watch out for her."

"I will. Don't worry," Zephyr said.

He nodded, and Era reached up on tiptoes to kiss him once more. He stood straight, threw his shoulders back, and boarded the transport.

Era wiped the tears from her eyes as the transport door closed. The alarm sounded again, and the hangar bay workers ordered everyone to leave.

"Come on. We have to go," Zephyr said quietly.

Era followed the rest of the family members out of the hangar bay and turned to watch the doors slide closed behind them. The transport started up on the other side, and the metal doors vibrated in response.

He's going to be fine. He'll come back. He always comes back. But the tears came anyway, spilling down her cheeks. None of her thoughts could erase the dread that had taken root in her stomach. Because some primal part of her knew.

She was never going to see Dritan again.

CHAPTER NINE

Era gripped the edge of the archivist station, the holo interface blurring before her. Six days. Dritan had been on Soren for six days. One hundred forty-four days left to go. Her limbs ached, and her mind felt dull from exhaustion. Each night she'd woken, gasping for breath. The empty womb, blood on the landing, being sucked into space...her nightmare made her fear sleep.

She tried to focus on what Mali was showing her on the stationary, but her eyes drifted to the colonists waiting to record messages for loved ones. Several couples, one little girl. Quiet, not engaged in conversation like they usually were. The change she'd sensed in the ship since the traitors were airlocked lingered everywhere.

In every sector, there were fewer words spoken, cut-off conversations, and more suspicious glances. Or maybe she was just seeing tension because of how she felt every minute of every day.

"Did you hear what I said?" Mali asked.

She stepped in front of Era. The holo shimmered, and the long list of commands merged with Mali's clothing and skin.

Era twisted a wrist, and her eyepiece shut off, removing the nausea-inducing image.

"Do you need some time, child?"

"No. Sorry."

Mali raised her eyebrows. "Dritan's doing his job, and we're doing ours. Being an archivist is important. I need to know you're ready for this."

"I am. I'm ready."

Mali shifted her gaze to some point beyond Era. Era turned, half-expecting to see Zephyr. But it was only Chief Petroff, making his way to the station.

Mali had moved Zephyr to first shift, said she needed to train with other techs since Era would be too busy now. But someone else on second shift could've trained Zephyr. It seemed more about keeping Era from distraction than about training Zephyr. Era only got to see her during mess and midbreak now.

Chief Petroff reached the station and set down a large metal case and an archive case. "Comms and an order from the board."

Comms. Was it too soon for there to be one from Dritan?

Mali opened the archive case. Inside were the archive cubes from the last order, plus an additional cube, set off to the side. The new cube order.

Mali took the guard's shift card, scanned it into the stationary, and handed it back. She popped the cube order into the slot on the stationary. "Is this urgent? I'm training her. It'll take me a little longer to get everything today."

Chief Petroff grunted. "I'll be back by shift's end for the order," he said and walked off.

"I expect you'll be granted access to the archives any day now. But until then, we'll work on the stationary," Mali said.

Era reactivated her eyepiece and tried to concentrate on the gestures Mali made as she moved through the system, but she couldn't pull her eyes from the comm case.

"As soon as I show you this, you can sort through those cubes. But right now, I need you to pay attention."

"Sorry." *Focus, Era.*

The cube order appeared on the holo. It contained a short list of numbers and letters, followed by descriptions.

"The numbers and letters on each line are the codes for specific cubes in the archives. The descriptions contain keywords for information they want us to find that they don't have the codes for."

Mali gestured and pulled up a search grid next to the words and used her index finger to draw one line of search terms into the grid. "You can drag the terms or say 'new entry' to search manually."

Theory; Artificial Environments; Dome construction; Blueprints.

Era's breath caught in her throat. Artificial environments? Dome construction? Did this have something to do with Soren?

Mali hit scan, and a new list appeared.

"The first cube code usually matches the query best, but not always," Mali pointed to the top code on the list. "So we send that one up first. If executive sends down for more

112

information, we send them the next relevant matches, in order."

"Why would they be searching for—?"

"Era," Mali said, her voice low. "You do not discuss what you see here. Not ever. Cube orders are confidential. Our job is not to analyze why they call up these cubes. Our job is to care for the archives and no more."

"I understand. But—as an archivist, have you ever...looked at one of the archive cubes?"

Mali rubbed the back of her neck. "Only in very rare instances and only with prior approval. Though we do have access to cubes that relate to our archivist duties."

Mali cocked her head to the side, considering Era. "Every time a cube from the archive is accessed," she said carefully, "it logs an eyepiece signature to show who accessed it."

Era swallowed. "I understand."

Mali held her gaze for a moment and nodded. "Good."

She brought up the cube order again, the keywords replaced by a list of codes. She pulled the order from the stationary and pushed it into the slot on her handheld. Then, she picked up the archive case. "While I return these and get the new order, you sort the comms and label them like I showed you."

"Can I—"

"If you find one from your husband, you can look at it. I won't make you wait." Mali headed for the archives.

Era grabbed the comm case and unlatched it. Eleven containers lay within. The twelfth space was empty. It would have held comms for executive sector. The rest of the containers were labeled with the names of each of the ten dekas and Soren: all the places messages could come from or be sent to. Era reached for the container labeled Soren.

Something turned over within her womb, and her hand flew to her stomach. Then another small movement, more obvious this time. *The baby.*

She'd almost convinced herself she hadn't felt anything that day in helio sector, that it had just been her imagination. But there it was again, the fluttering sensation.

The Defect is a lie.

Era's amnio results were probably ready by now, but she hadn't gathered the courage to go to Medlevel and schedule her appointment. She couldn't put it off much longer. Zephyr

114

said she'd go with her, but that didn't make any of it more bearable.

Era took a deep breath and glanced at the holo. The search results were gone now, but the holo was still logged into the search grid. She really should turn it off and begin sorting the comm cubes like Mali had asked her, but what the traitor had said...

She took a quick look around to make sure she was still alone. Mali had entered the archives, and only a few colonists waited on the benches to record messages.

She tapped the grid.

"New entry," she whispered. "The Defect. Legacy Code."

The words appeared on the entry line, and Era selected scan to begin the search. A long list of cube codes appeared, and Era's pulse quickened.

What was she even hoping to find? The Defect wasn't a lie. The Defect from the Legacy Code was real, and here were all the files to prove it.

Era memorized the first result, repeating it over and over until it stuck. *CD-1dy34b.*

She accessed the program's memory core and wiped her search. What was she thinking, looking this stuff up? What was the point, when she couldn't access the cubes anyway?

Era picked up the container labeled Soren. At least three dozen cubes lay within. If Dritan had the chance to record a message, he would've. And she really needed to see his face and hear his voice right now.

∞

She found his message halfway through the stack. His still holo image made her heart hurt. His features were downcast, and his shoulders slumped. He didn't look like the man she'd kissed good-bye. And this message would've been recorded as soon as he'd landed. How bad was it down there?

She hadn't been close to anyone who'd been there, but she'd glimpsed those who'd come back to the *London* after the first draft. She'd heard their stories, second-hand: cave-ins, malfunctioning air purifiers, tainted water supplies, accidents with machinery. Many workers from the first draft had broken bodies and were nothing more than a burden to the fleet.

The survivors had stayed on their levels,

rarely venturing upward. She'd seen them during her brief visits with Dritan in the sublevels. But *all* the survivors, visibly broken or not, wore haunted expressions, as if the people they'd lost on Soren still visited them at night, stealing their sleep. When Dritan came back, would he look like that? If Dritan came back...

Era's stomach flipped, and she reached for a handheld under the station. She took Dritan's comm cube from the stationary and sank to the floor behind the desk. No one needed to watch her cry. The tears were already coming, and she hadn't even started the holovid yet.

She tapped the file and splayed her fingers wide, palm out, to launch it.

Dritan's face appeared, and she involuntarily reached for him. Her hand passed through the holo, causing it to shimmer, and the pressure in her throat intensified.

Dark circles lined Dritan's eyes, but he was still as handsome as ever. The scene behind him could've been the scene from inside any cubic, but the panels were clean and undented. If only the shiny, new cubic wasn't deep underground on a toxic planet.

117

He cleared his throat. "Name: Dritan Corinth. Message for: Era Corinth. Destination: *Paragon.*" He smiled, but it looked false. "I only get a minute. I miss you, and I love you. I can't wait to see you again. I hope things are okay up there."

Dritan paused and ran a hand through his tight black curls. He leaned closer to the vidrelay. "By the time you get this, you'll probably know the test results. Whatever they are, it'll be okay," he said forcefully, as if saying the words would make them true. "I wish I could be there for you. Let me know what's happening."

Tears slid down Era's face, but she didn't wipe them away.

Dritan seemed to want to say more, but he shot a glance past the vidrelay, where the witness would have been sitting.

"I'm staying safe. It's great down here. Plenty of food. Everything works. I love you." The holo blanked.

She pressed her lips together and watched the vid again. She needed to find out her test results and send him an answer. He deserved to know. He didn't need to be worrying while he was doing his job.

118

Era wiped her face, sniffed, and got to her feet. She turned, searching for Mali, and saw her leaving the storage cubic. Era straightened.

She only had one more day to record a message for Dritan before the next shipment of cubes went out from the *Paragon*. She couldn't put it off any longer. She should've gone two days ago to schedule her appointment on medlevel.

Mali walked up to the archivist station. "Did you get a message?"

Era nodded and rested her hand on her belly. "I need to make an appointment on medlevel. They had to give me an amnio. My results are probably ready. He'll want to know what they are..."

Mali rested a hand on Era's arm. "I'm sure he will. Why don't you leave a little early today? Take care of what you need to."

Had Mali had a failed pregnancy, too? Probably. Era had never heard her speak about any children. She took off her eyepiece and gave it to Mali. "Thank you."

This was it. She'd schedule her appointment, and then she'd know.

She'd either be bringing new life into the fleet, or...

No point considering the alternative.

CHAPTER TEN

Era stepped up to the population management station and swiped her card.

The same girl from last time stood behind the station. Era drew a deep breath to steady herself. "The medic said I had to schedule an appointment."

The clerk splayed her fingers wide and tapped the air. "Era Corinth. Ah. Your test results are ready."

Era shifted her stance and fought the urge to walk out. She'd try to schedule her appointment for midbreak tomorrow, when she and Zephyr would both be free. She didn't want to do this alone, not any more than she'd wanted to do it alone last time.

"Medic Faust can see you now," the clerk said.

"What? I...I have to go to mess. Can I do it tomorrow?"

"No. Your appointment is flagged priority. And no one's scheduled this block." The clerk moved around the station and headed toward the corridor.

Priority? That was bad, wasn't it? Why would she be flagged priority if they had good news for her?

Get it over with so Dritan can stop worrying. So you can stop wondering.

She struggled to keep her breathing even as she followed the clerk back to a cubic.

The clerk left. Era sat down on a stool and tapped her foot on the ground. She pressed her hands to her swollen belly and stared at the floor, willing herself to stay calm. Her mind wandered to the bare shelf in her cubic, to the pale green scrap of bedding folded there. Would they get the chance to wrap their newborn in it?

The buzzer sounded, calling an end to second shift and announcing the beginning of last mess.

Medic Faust en- tered, looking tired

122

and older than she'd seemed just a week before. She sat down on a stool by the curved
cabinets, a hard expression on her face, hands
folded in her lap. Era's shoulders caved in, and
her stomach twisted on itself.

"I'm sorry. The cells have markers for the
Defect."

Era choked back a small sob, her hands
slipping from her stomach.

Defective.

All the things she'd let herself dream about
in the past few weeks, all the hope she'd had
for the future. Gone.

Medic Faust's lined face blurred in front of
her, and Era leaned forward. The metal panels
of the cubic seemed to grow closer, shutting
her in.

"Your abort session will be two days from
now. First shift, second block," the medic said,
not meeting Era's eyes. "Dritan can attend.
You'll have a few free days afterward for recu-
peration."

Era's eyes focused on the medic's hard face.
"Dritan's on Soren," she whispered.

Medic Faust paled and rubbed her forehead.
"I'd like to get you going on some grimp," she
said. She stood and opened a cabinet.

Grimp. The sound of the medic rifling through the cabinet took on a strange muffled quality, and a cold feeling spread through Era, starting at her throat and traveling down into her limbs.

Era rose to her feet and balled her hands into fists. "The Defect is a lie." The words tumbled from her mouth before she could stop them.

Medic Faust froze, and Era searched her face. But her expression was a blank mask and gave away nothing.

"Is it? Is it a lie?" Era's voice cracked. "One of the traitors said it was."

The medic's eyes widened slightly, and she pressed her lips together. She took a step away from Era and placed the grimp back on the counter with a shaking hand. "The cells in your womb carry the Defect. I see you're upset. I understand. But you should know better than to repeat the words of a traitor. You know what happened to the traitors. I won't report this, but you need to forget what you heard him say."

"It's not just cells. I felt it move."

The medic picked up the pills. "I want you

to start on these. Once daily. They'll help."

Something wasn't right, but this entire experience was beginning to feel holo, more like a nightmare than anything that could really be happening. "You didn't answer my question."

"I'll see you in two days. If I hear you talk like that again, I will have to report you." The medic shoved the pills into Era's hand and went to the door.

"What if I say no?"

"Say no?"

"What if I don't want to abort."

Medic Faust took a deep breath and met Era's gaze. "Disobeying population regulation is treason. I trust you don't want to experience the consequences of that."

She hit the button on the door and gestured for Era to leave.

As Era passed through the doorway, the old medic gripped her shoulder with one bony hand. "You're young enough to get another chance. The next one could be viable."

Era narrowed her eyes. "'A better world awaits.' Doesn't it?"

Medic Faust pursed her lips and released Era's arm.

Era placed her hand against her stomach and hurried away, not knowing where she was going, only knowing she needed to get as far away from this level as she could.

∞

She took the stairs two at a time, not sure where she was fleeing to. A few colonists flashed her dark looks as she pushed past, but she didn't slow down until she reached the top of the stairs. Observation.

It'd be empty during last mess, so close to curfew, but maybe...maybe Zephyr would be here. She wouldn't have stayed in the galley for long without Era.

The blood-red planet filled the expanse, impassive as ever about its role in humanity's survival.

Dritan was down there somewhere. Era's eyes burned, and she moved forward, searching for Zephyr's familiar head of red-blond hair.

Zephyr sat in front of the glass, but she wasn't alone. Tadeo sat beside her, his head tilted toward her. He smiled at something she said and leaned clos-   er.

Era's stomach twisted. Tadeo didn't need to know her baby was defective. And Zephyr didn't need her night ruined. Little enough happiness in this fleet.

Era strode to the furthest empty corner of the observation deck. She collapsed on the floor and pressed against the hard metal wall. She still clutched the plastic packet of grimp in her hand, and she let it slide to the floor beside her.

Grimp would dull the pain, but it felt wrong to dull her senses—to avoid feeling the pain she should feel. *Did* feel.

This blackness felt like deep space, a place with no warmth, and no hope of life or light ahead. Soren blurred in her vision as the tears finally came.

At least her baby wouldn't have to suffer a lifetime on Soren. She pressed both hands against her stomach and closed her eyes. Her own body had betrayed her, formed a baby who couldn't survive.

My baby. Never just a 'collection of non-sentient cells.' In two days, I'll cast you into a world that would have killed you even if I'd carried you longer.

"I'm so sorry," Era whispered.

The ancestors deserved what they got for what they did to humanity.

No one ever talked about what it was like to have to abort. Was it this excruciating for others, or did she have an abnormal attachment to this—to the baby—within her?

Of course, it had to be done. There was no use carrying it to term. The lungs and heart would be wrong, deformed. It'd be born into the world and suffocate before taking its first breath. Letting it come to term was cruel and a waste of the extra food and water she'd consume.

The regulation was there to protect the living. She'd been so naive to let herself feel love for this baby before knowing if it had the Defect.

She rubbed the rough fabric over her stomach and swallowed against the pain in her throat. *But would you really die? Is everything I know about the Defect true?*

Era's gaze focused on the jumpgate.

CD-1dy34b. The cube with the Legacy Code history on it.

Accessing the records would be treason, and she couldn't get to them anyway, even if she was willing to commit the crime.

And she wasn't. She wouldn't betray Mali's trust.

Era Corinth. Traitor.

She let out a bitter laugh and wiped her face with her sleeve. Dritan told her to keep her head down. What would happen if the medic did report what Era said today? *How could I be so stupid?*

She took a deep breath, grabbed the grimp packet from the floor, and pushed to her feet.

Zephyr and Tadeo still sat in front of the expanse, huddled close on the bench.

Era pushed her thoughts of treason away, buried them deep. She had to abort, follow the law. Other women did it. They aborted and somehow survived. She'd survive too. What other option was there?

CHAPTER ELEVEN

Era spooned some quin gruel into her mouth and tried to swallow it. *So tired.* She'd had the nightmare again last night. Maybe her mind had been trying to warn her this whole time she'd have to abort.

She looked down at the sad, half-ration of gruel she'd been given, dropped the spoon into her bowl, and searched the galley for Zephyr. Era found her at the end of the line, taking a steaming bowl and cup from the galley worker's grasp. Zephyr stepped out of line and headed toward her.

"Sorry I missed you last night," she said as she slid onto the bench across from Era. She stared into her gruel, her spoon poised above it, a crooked half-smile on her lips. "I waited for you, but Tadeo wanted to meet up, and well, you know. He might've been hurt if I didn't show. Couldn't disappoint him."

Zephyr wrinkled her nose and lifted a spoonful of the gruel. She let the coagulated mass slide back into the bowl. "But—ugh. I might have to stop seeing him if he keeps talking about the president like she's some kind of old Earth Goddess."

Era extended her arms in front of her, hands in fists, and closed her eyes. If there ever were any gods, they'd turned their backs on humanity a long time ago. She took a deep breath and opened her eyes.

"By the way, you're wrong about him. He *definitely* likes girls—" Zephyr looked at Era and her brow creased with concern. "I did wait for you, you know, at least—for a little while—"

"I was at medlevel," Era said.

Zephyr's eyes widened, and she reached across the table to grip Era's hand. "I said I'd come with you."

Era shook her head and forced the words out. "I have to abort."

Zephyr's eyes darted to the colonists on either side of them. "I'm sorry," she said in a low voice. "I didn't know."

Era's stomach turned inside out, and she tucked a strand of hair behind her ear.

"When? When do you have to do it?"

"Tomorrow. First shift. Second block." Era wanted to tell Zephyr what she'd been thinking about the Defect. She wanted to tell her what she'd heard the traitor say, but she couldn't, not here in the galley. And what good would it do anyway?

"You want me to come with you?" Zephyr asked. "I will. I'm coming. Mali'll let me."

Era nodded slightly and drew her arm away from Zephyr.

The loud chatter in the galley died to a whisper, and Era looked up, seeking the reason. She found it. A group of guards were pushing past people waiting in the mess line.

The guards spread out and began walking through the galley, past each table, searching, just like they had the day the traitor attacked Tesmee.

One of them walked by Era, and she held her breath, shrinking in her seat. She saw herself, reflected in his eyepiece, as his gaze swept over them.

His comcuff crackled. "Near Entrance B."

The guard strode toward the far end of the galley, and Era twisted on the bench to see what was happening.

Shouts echoed across the hushed space from the area where the sublevel workers sat. Where Dritan's crew used to sit. The guards hauled four colonists to their feet and led them toward the doors.

One of the workers, a half who looked fresh out of caretaker sector, pulled away from the guards. "I didn't mean it. I didn't mean what I said." His high-pitched voice rang out, and everyone craned their necks in his direction.

The guard closest to the boy reached for him, but the boy lurched away, running for the doors. Another guard darted after him and slammed a fist into the back of his head.

The boy went down, and Era sucked in a breath. Why would the president bother arresting a brand new half? What could he possibly have said or done to be a threat?

Two of the guards dragged the limp boy out of the galley with the rest of the prisoners. Several moments passed, and the chatter picked up again, more subdued than it had been.

Era stared into her gruel, her appetite

gone. This ship was supposed to be safer. The guards were supposed to be here to protect the colonists. Weren't they?

Zephyr slammed her spoon into her bowl. "So our president's arresting halfs now. She gonna send guards to caretaker sector next?"

Era took a drink of water to get rid of the sour taste in her mouth. She cupped her palms over her belly, too sick to eat, and waited for Zephyr to be done.

This will be gone after tomorrow. My baby will be gone.

She blinked to banish the tears springing up in her eyes. How would she get through this without Dritan? Zephyr didn't get it. She couldn't understand what this was like—not yet.

Era had thrown the grimp Medic Faust gave her on the shelf next to her bunk and hadn't given it a second thought. But right now, the promise of feeling nothing tempted her. Anything to get rid of this pain.

"*The president will what? Save us all? The president does what's good for the president.*" That's what Zephyr had said. But Era hadn't believed it. Now she didn't know what to believe.

Had she been naive to think the president had the fleet's best interests at heart? Had she been stupid to think this ship could be a chance at a better life in the fleet?

A movement pressed against her from within her womb. The tears filling her eyes poured over, and she wiped them away. *Not gonna cry. Not here.*

Era felt a light hand on her shoulder, and she looked up. Zephyr had finished and was standing next to her. "Dritan will come back," she said. "You'll try again."

I don't want to try again. I want this *baby.*

Era stood up and grabbed her bowl to take it back to the line. She dropped it into the bin and followed Zephyr out of the galley.

When they stepped into the corridor, Zephyr crossed her arms. "Tadeo wanted to meet up during midbreak, but we can—"

"No. You should be with him."

"But...I finished my song yesterday. We could go up to Observation..."

"I didn't sleep that great. I think I'm just going to go back to my cubic 'til my shift."

The buzzer went off, and a quiet group of techs exited the galley, followed by a crew of sublevel workers.

Zephyr gave Era a hug. The warm touch made Era's eyes fill again.

"You know Mali just wanted to get rid of me," she said. "I'm gonna find a way to get back on the same shift as you."

"Go, before you're late," Era said.

All she wanted to do was crawl back into her bunk, hug Dritan's pillow to her and inhale the quickly fading scent of him.

"See you at last mess?"

"Yeah. For sure," Era said.

Zephyr gave her a little wave and turned to go. She walked to the main stairwell, her chin held high, her long impractical red-blond hair swinging behind her. Defiant in a place steeped in too much fear.

I've never been defiant about anything.

Era pressed a fist against the swell of her stomach and headed the opposite way, for the stairwell that would drop her off closest to her cubic.

The Defect is a Lie.

Medic Faust had never answered her—had never said it wasn't.

Something broke free inside Era, and the tightness in her chest released.

I won't go through with the abortion.

She couldn't do it. Not without seeing the truth for herself, with her own eyes.

And she knew how she could access CD-1dy34b.

CHAPTER TWELVE

Era had never been very good at deception. By the time she reached the repository for her shift, her suit stuck to her in all the wrong places, and every beat of her heart felt like a dying helio banging against her ribcage.

Mali would see her and know what Era was planning. How could she not?

A large crowd had gathered in the waiting area, and Era realized, with a start, that comms were going out today.

Mali stood at the comm station, helping an older worker, a man whose name Era didn't know. Mali handed holo gear to a waiting colonist and smiled when she saw Era walking through the doors.

"Do we have an order today?" Era tried to say it like she didn't care, but failed.

"No, not yet."

Era's muscles relaxed. Her plan hinged on being here when the cube order came in. But could she really do it? Could she really betray Mali?

Mali's eyes drifted to Era's stomach, then she met Era's gaze.

You didn't pry into the status of someone else's pregnancy. Mali wouldn't ask her about it, and Era didn't trust herself to talk about it without blurting out her plan. "Where do you want me today?"

"Transport's going out. I'm about to help witness." Mali tilted her head toward the table where Paige and Helice sat, two comm cases in front of them. "They're handling incoming and outgoing, but we're short on handhelds."

Era repressed a sigh. She'd have to record a message for Dritan. What would she say? How could she say it?

"I'll fix handhelds." Era swiped her card across the scanner.

Mali logged an eyepiece in and handed it to her. "I'll be witnessing if you need me."

Era nodded and walked to storage. As

140

she retrieved the bin of holos, her eyes drifted to the empty archive cube cases, and her heart sped up.

If the chief brought an order today, she'd add the Legacy Code cube to it. But there were too many things she had to do to ensure she didn't get caught. So many places where things could go wrong.

She didn't carry the bin to a cubic. Instead, she chose a table near the archivist station. She had to be close by if an order came. There'd only be one chance.

Era worked on the handhelds, glancing up every so often toward the doors. She'd finished her fifth handheld when Chief Petroff walked in.

She clutched the next handheld in one sticky palm and gestured to make it seem like she was working.

"Excuse me," the chief said.

Era deactivated her eyepiece and looked up. The chief stood next to her table, an archive case in his hand.

"I have an order for Mali." He lowered his brow.

Era's stomach dropped, and she licked her lips. "She's witnessing messages."

"Can you get her?" He said it slowly, dragging each word out like he thought she was some worthless half.

Mali would reprimand Era for this, but what was this against the treason she was about to commit? She wiped her palms down her suit.

"I'm busy right now," she said.

The chief's face reddened, and Era reactivated her eyepiece. He grunted and walked off.

Era waited a moment, her mouth drier than quin flatbread, then stood and walked over to the archivist station. She tried to act natural, but every movement felt stiff.

The chief was talking to Paige now. Paige glanced her way and pointed to one of the recording cubics.

Hurry. Sweat sprung up on Era's forehead as she gestured to activate her eyepiece and connect it with the stationary's display module. She pulled the diagnostic out and hooked it to the stationary.

It took her less than a minute to locate the line of code she'd fixed a week earlier, the one that had caused the interface to go blank on Mali. She rewrote it, changing it back to the infinite loop glitch.

Mali had exited the recording cubic and was speaking with Chief Petroff.

Era's stomach turned as she made a fist to close out the code and gestured to deactivate her eyepiece. She shoved the diagnostic under the station and stepped back just as Mali and the chief started walking toward her.

Era put her hands behind her and took several deep breaths. Had Mali seen her? *What's my excuse for why I'm standing here and not fixing handhelds? What would Zephyr say?*

Mali drew closer and narrowed her eyes. "Era, please come get me next time."

"I...I will. I'm sorry." Era focused on her scuffed boots.

Why am I here, why am I here, why am I here?

"I just wanted to find out how many working handhelds you need." *Lame.*

Mali's brow wrinkled. "I need as many as you can fix."

Chief Petroff gave Mali his shift card and the archive case. Mali swiped his card and handed it back.

"When do you need this by?" Mali asked.

"I'll be back at the end of shift."

"We'll have it for you."

Chief Petroff's steely gaze landed on Era again, and he headed for the door. She turned back to the table and clasped her hands over her stomach in a failed effort to stop it from churning.

Mali swore under her breath. "Era. There's that glitch again. How long will it take you to fix it? I hope I don't need to go chase Chief Petroff down for his card."

"Depends on what kind of glitch it is." She barely heard the sound of her own voice over the rush of her pulse.

Mali sighed. "Try to get it working. I'll go return these."

Mali walked toward the archives, and Era's shoulders caved, all the tension in her giving way to fear and guilt. Maybe she was better at this deception thing than she thought.

She attached her eyepiece to the system and fixed the glitch.

When she finished, she took a quick look around. Still alone. No one paying attention to her.

She accessed the cube order. Two files appeared. The order and a request for personnel files. She set her jaw and tapped the cube order.

"New entry," she whispered.

A blinking dot appeared at the bottom of the list.

"CD-1dy34b."

She released a slow breath when the code appeared in the slot. The subject material probably didn't match whatever else executive had ordered, so she dragged it higher on the list. With luck, Mali wouldn't notice the anomaly.

Era closed the file out, then accessed the memory core to delete her eyepiece signature and the fact that she'd added an entry to the cube.

She'd try to get back in here and delete the addition later, but she couldn't worry about that now. Its presence on the list would be a mystery. An accidental add-on. She doubted they would even notice this extra cube.

"Is it done?" Mali said.

Era gripped the station, and her hands slipped down the edge, damp with sweat. Mali stood next to her, had appeared without Era hearing her approach.

"It's fixed." Era disconnected her eyepiece and the diagnostic from the display module, and Mali checked her work.

"Looks like a simple cube pull and data search," Mali said. "I can handle this. I really need those handhelds."

"I'll get back to it." Era hurried away without waiting for a response.

She watched furtively as Mali fetched the case from storage and brought it into the archives.

Would Mali notice the cube she'd added, suspect something wasn't right? *Breathe.* She tried to focus on the handheld she was attempting to fix, but her brain wouldn't cooperate.

Mali finally exited the archives with the case and took it straight to storage. Era felt the flush in her cheeks, the sweat dripping down her back.

This thrill was new. It had an edge, yet filled her with a kind of wild, terrifying relief. She'd broken the rules, and no one had noticed.

Once she fixed the other handhelds, she'd take the bin back to storage.

And then she'd learn the truth.

∞

Era pushed a working handheld to the side of the table and picked up the next one. Some glitch in the system kept the interface from loading. She wiped the sweat from her forehead and connected the diagnostic. The only way to fix this was to start over, delete everything. She reset the system to its original settings and loaded a fresh copy of the main program.

The interface reappeared, and Era tested it. Everything worked.

Sometimes the tech just needed a new copy of the program—a new chance to function smoothly.

The time on her eyepiece told her she only had two hours left until the end of shift.

I can't do it.

Why had she done something so stupid? If they found out now, would they call it treason? They might take away her clearance, switch her job, but she hadn't accessed the cube yet. It wasn't too late to back out, to forget she ever did any of this and hope no one up in executive noticed the extra cube in the case.

"How many do we have?" Mali said from beside her.

Era dropped the handheld.

"You feeling alright?"

"I'm okay."

"Chief Petroff will be back soon for the pull and comms. I want you to help me witness."

Era picked up the handheld she'd just fixed and pointed to the pile off to the side of the table. "I got those working. I'll take the rest back to storage."

Era dropped the working handheld into the bin and hefted it into her arms. She carried it back to storage, bile inching further up her throat with each step. She swiped her card, and the door slid open. The lume bar illuminated the compartment, and Era stepped inside.

The door slid closed behind her, and she pushed the bin onto the shelf. Only then did she allow herself to look at the archive cases on the shelf below. The case on top would contain the cube she'd added.

I can't do it. I won't. She stood taller and exhaled. It wasn't too late to stop this. What would Dritan say if he knew what she'd already done?

She walked back to the door and leaned against the panel beside it, pressing her forehead to the cool met- al. *But I'll be aborting*

148

our baby without ever knowing the truth. And the truth's here. How long before I get another chance to see it?

She groaned and focused on the panel in front of her. She popped it off and scrutinized the underlying circuitry.

There it was. The wire that always gave Dritan and her so much trouble in their cubic. She never thought she'd be locking herself in on purpose.

She disconnected the wire and hit the button next to the door to be sure her sabotage had worked. The door didn't open.

Every muscle in her body screamed at her to get out of the cubic, give this up, but she licked her lips and walked to the shelf. She plunged her hand into the bin and retrieved the handheld she'd fixed.

She placed it on the floor and pulled the archive case from the shelf.

Once I do this, there's no going back.

Era took a deep breath and opened the case.

CHAPTER THIRTEEN

The line of silver cubes looked exactly like any other collection of cubes, except for the tiny numbers engraved into the sides of each of them. Era leaned in, squinting, and searched for the right cube.

It should be somewhere in the middle of the group, if Mali had stored them in order.

CD-1dy34b.

She picked it up and pushed it into the handheld before she could change her mind. Once she activated her eyepiece, the cube would store her shift card information in its memory core. But she should be able to delete it, even if the memory core had security measures in place.

The Defect is a lie.

Let's see if it is. She turned the handheld on and twisted her wrist.

Rows of files appeared on the cube—too many for Era to search through. Her hand trembled as she tapped the first one and splayed her fingers wide to bring it up.

A holovid shimmered into existence, and Era recoiled.

The woman before her was ancient, older than anyone she'd ever seen. Watery brown eyes peered out from wrinkled, sagging skin. Was this a woman from Earth? People used to live longer, before life on the fleet put an end to that.

The woman cleared her throat.

"Name: Avia Sherman, Infinitek Lead Scientist, Genetic Research. This is the official reference file for genetic modification 2672 at allele rs120893068. The modification is heritable, appearing in half of all fetuses. It results..."

Avia's voice cracked and she cleared her throat.

"It results in serious heart and lung defects. Early attempts to repair the defective gene have met with little to no success. The only way to increase the lifespan of affected newborns is through heart and lung sur-

152

gery. Three in five newborns survive the surgeries. Long-term prognosis unknown. Chances of survival are greater with proper care and resources. If facilities or resources not available..."

Avia closed her eyes for a moment. When she opened them, she raised a hand. "Abortion recommended." She made a fist, and the holo went blank.

Era rocked back on her heels and sank against the metal shelf, unable to keep her balance. She wrapped both hands around the swell of her belly.

Not hopeless, like they'd said.

The Defect wasn't a lie. But they'd all been lied to. Her baby had a chance, could live. How many women had aborted children who could've survived if only they'd been given the chance?

Heat rose in Era's cheeks, and she clenched her hands into fists. The fluttering in her belly happened more frequently now. She hadn't imagined the movements and couldn't deny their existence any longer. Her baby was not just a collection of cells. How could she abort, now that she knew her baby had a chance?

What operations needed to be done? Could the medics here on the *Paragon* do them? They had the space, the medics, the drugs they made on zero deck...

Era gestured, intent on opening the next file. A beep went off outside the door and she froze. Mali was trying to access the storage cubic.

Era jerked her hand in a gesture to bring up the cube's memory core. Her pulse roared in her ears as she located the access data, found her eyepiece signature, and tried to wipe the last entry. The interface flickered, malfunctioning, and blanked. She was locked out of the program.

The door beeped again, and a faint voice called from the other side of it.

Era sucked in a breath and tried to slow her heart down. "The door's stuck." Her voice came out too soft, so she repeated it, louder this time.

Mali replied, her words muffled.

Era couldn't leave this cubic until she'd erased the evidence of her treason. How long did she have before Mali called up a maintenance crew to force open the door?

She stood on shaky legs and

gripped the edge of the holo gear bin. It slid through her hands and crashed to the floor. The sound of it seemed impossibly loud in the small space, and it paralyzed her. Mali called out again.

Move, Era. Focus.

She righted the bin and grabbed the diagnostic from where it had fallen on the tile. She knelt down next to the frozen handheld and hooked the diagnostic in.

The code came up in her eyepiece, and she scanned it, seeking the error.

There.

Another knock on the door.

"I'm trying to open it from in here. I'm working on it." Era yelled the words, but they sounded like they came from someone else. Her brain was trying to untangle the broken code before her. She let her mind take over and rewrote the code, fixing the bug. The handheld's interface reappeared.

She inhaled ragged breaths, brought up the archive cube once more, and accessed the memory core.

She gestured to delete her eyepiece signature. A warning appeared.

Unauthorized Command.

Era narrowed her eyes. Unauthorized didn't mean inaccessible. She'd expected this, hadn't she?

She tried another method. That one failed, too.

Mali yelled something. It sounded like a question.

"I think I figured it out." Era closed her eyes. "One minute."

I think I figured it out.

Era tried accessing the memory core using another trick, a hack her father had taught her for when the ship's systems malfunctioned and rendered memory core data inaccessible. It could damage the data, but what other choice did she have?

The memory core came up, and Era tried once more to delete her eyepiece signature.

It worked.

She bit off a giddy laugh, double-checked the memory core to be sure her signature was gone, and ripped the cube from the handheld.

She dropped the cube into the archive case, ensured it lined up the way Mali had stored it, and placed it back on the shelf.

The handhelds were still scattered across the floor. Heart pounding, she scooped them up, dumped them in the bin, and shoved it back on the shelf.

Her hands were damp, and they slipped along the wire's plastic coating as she reconnected it. She clumsily slid the panel in place and stepped away from it.

The door opened. Mali met Era's gaze, and Era stiffened.

What have I done?

It was over. Mali would know, would have to suspect. A cold chill took root in Era, and she placed her hands behind her back, pressing closer to the shelf.

I committed treason. The penalty for treason is—

"What happened?"

"The door jammed. And just now—it finally opened. I don't know what happened." The words rushed out, the sound of them too bright, *false.*

Mali pressed the inner button to keep the door from sliding shut on them. "I was getting ready to call the maintenance crew up...Oh. Come child, no more tears. Wipe your face, now."

Era nodded dumbly and wiped at her damp cheeks. When had she started crying?

Did Mali really trust her so much that she didn't suspect anything? That she couldn't see the obvious?

Mali gave her a kindly smile. Era sniffed and forced her legs to move, to propel her out of storage.

She'd done it. She'd committed treason and hadn't gotten caught. They would never know she looked at the cube.

But now that she knew the truth, what would she do with it?

∞

Era followed Mali to the recording station and picked up one of the handhelds, a vidrelay, and a handful of blank comm cubes to record messages on.

The Defect can be fixed.

"Eight is empty." Mali pointed to a recording cubic at the far end of the wall.

Era waved a waiting colonist over and led him to the compartment. She set up the vidrelay, then activated her handheld and eyepiece. "Where's this going?"

The man sat down. "The *London*."

Three in five infants   survive the surgeries.

Era retreated to her own chair across the table from him, tapped the holo between the vidrelay rods, and gestured to start the recording.

My baby might live.

The man began to speak, but his words melded together, became meaningless. He could be making plans for another riot right now, and she wouldn't have noticed. Or cared.

What would happen when she refused to abort? Because she couldn't go along with it. Not now.

What would Medic Faust do? Did she know the truth? How could the woman perform abortions if she did?

Era squeezed her hands in her lap.

She'd have to admit she knew an operation could fix her baby. Only she couldn't admit that, because then they'd know she'd looked at the archives. And then they'd know who added the cube to the order.

How could she save her child without giving away her treason? Some deep part of her had believed everything she'd ever been taught about the Defect. She'd never considered what she'd do if the traitor turned out to be *right*.

The enormity of the truth settled within her, and she shivered.

The man cleared his throat, finished now, and she shut off the vidrelay. She rose to her feet and walked him to the door. He left the cubic, but Era didn't call the next person in. She stole a glance around the waiting area. Paige and Helice were engrossed in a conversation, and no one else looked her way.

She closed the door and pressed her back against it, staring at the scuffed metal panels across from her. She'd tell Medic Faust what she knew and ask her to save her child. If the medic refused to save her baby, she'd threaten to tell the fleet the truth about the Defect. It was the only thing she had to bargain with.

But could she really keep this secret in exchange for her own baby's survival? The rest of the fleet would have to know sometime. Her stomach twisted.

She'd patch that panel when it failed. She had to save her own baby first. If she couldn't even do that, how could she help anyone else?

But if she gave the medic that ultimatum, threatened to spill their secret, they'd arrest her and airlock her. She needed a back-up plan. She didn't want to involve Zephyr, but she couldn't do this alone.

Era clenched her hands into fists and stumbled back to the table. She knew what she had to do.

Technically, she needed a witness to watch her record a message to Dritan. But what was one more law broken after what she'd done today? What she planned to do?

Era sat where the colonist had and dropped his cube next to her. She took a new, blank cube and pushed it into the handheld.

What should she tell Dritan? She couldn't tell him everything, but she had to tell him something. In case it all went wrong.

She sat up straight, tapped the vidrelay holo and began the recording. Her eyepiece would give away the fact that she had no witness, that she was recording her own message, so she took it off and set it aside.

"Name: Era Corinth. Message for: Dritan Corinth. Destination: Soren."

She paused and waited a full minute to begin speaking. Whoever sorted cubes down on Soren didn't need to hear any part of her message.

"I know you've been waiting on news from me. Our baby...our baby has the Defect. But I found out something else, something I shouldn't have. I wish I could tell you more, but I can't. Not like this.

"I'm sorry I have to do what I'm about to do, and that it might cause trouble for you, but...I have to. Please don't be worried about me. I miss you every day."

Era pressed her lips together and tried to look confident. She should tell him he'd hear from her soon, that she was planning to save their baby, but pulling Zephyr into this was bad enough. She wouldn't drag Dritan into it too. Zephyr's father might be able to protect her, but who would protect Dritan? He'd end up airlocked, like his crew members. The less he knew, the better.

"I love you," she said. She put the eyepiece back on and gestured to turn off the vidrelay. For the first time in months, her body felt light. The heavy weight she hadn't realized she'd been carrying was gone. This plan was crazy, terrifying even, but it was a *plan*.

Era accessed the holovid she'd recorded and clipped it, deleting the parts where she'd worn her eyepiece.

She took the cube from the handheld, set it off to the side, and inserted a blank one.

Someone's gonna walk in on me.

But she couldn't risk locking herself in a cubic twice in one day. Not when she'd already been caught once. She'd have to take her chances.

Era sat up straight, cleared her throat, and hit record. She didn't bother removing her eyepiece. No need to hide her treason this time.

"My name is Era Corinth...and I'm a traitor. I illegally accessed the archives, but I hope that once I share what I learned, you can forgive my treason.

"What we've been told about the Defect is a lie. The truth about the Defect can be found on archive cube CD-1dy34b. Three out of five defective newborns can be saved through surgery. Our children don't have to be aborted."

Era paused, letting her truth sink in for her imaginary audience.

"I'm recording this comm as a fail-safe. I intend to ask my medic on the *Paragon* to save my child. I believe there's a good chance they'll charge me with treason once they realize what I've done. But I have to try to save my baby."

The words caught in Era's throat, and she had to close her eyes and take a deep breath before continuing.

"If they charge me—if they prevent me from sharing what I've found—I will ensure my discoveries are shared with the fleet. In fact, if you're watching this now, I probably failed to save my child. But with this knowledge...you might be able to save yours."

Era stared into the vidrelay for a moment longer, then shut it off. She pulled out the cube and strode to the far wall. This wasn't something she could carry around with her. She popped one of the panels off and nestled her fail-safe in a jumble of wires.

A recording cubic had to be near the bottom of any maintenance priority list. And who would ever think she'd hide it in the very room she'd recorded it in? No one would be looking for this here. No one except Zephyr, if the worst came to pass.

She reattached the panel and picked up Dritan's comm cube in one hand and the colonist's comm in the other.

A flutter passed through her belly. Whether it was the baby or her own renewed hope, she didn't know. It didn't matter. She had a plan. She had a way to save her child and a way to protect herself if things didn't go well.

This could work. It had to.

Era exited the recording cubic and headed straight for the table where Paige and Helice sat collecting comms.

Paige looked up and scowled. She stood, the outgoing message case in her grasp. "I'm done sorting. Sorry. You're too late. The chief is here."

Era's hand went to her belly. Chief Petroff stood in front of the archivist station's high counter, gripping the archive cube case. Mali worked behind the station, her eyepiece activated. Zephyr stood by her side, her face drawn and pale. *Zephyr?*

Era's scalp prickled, and time seemed to slow. Why was Zephyr here? "I'm taking the case to Mali."

Helice fidgeted in her chair, looking at Paige.

Paige narrowed her eyes. "Just because you—"

Enough of this glitch. Era wrenched the case from Paige's grasp and slammed it down on the table. She flipped open the lid and dropped her cube to Dritan into the Soren container and the colonist's cube in the container for the *London*.

"Mali will—"

"I'm taking it." Era closed the case and yanked it away as Paige reached out to grab it.

Era started toward the archivist station and froze. Zephyr was staring at her, eyes wide, lips slightly parted. Mali's somber attention was directed at something only she could see on the stationary's holo.

The air around Era seemed to gather a charge, and her legs grew heavy, like someone had dialed up the grav system.

Her body begged her to run the other way, but her legs took her forward, toward a scene that made no sense. Something was very wrong. *They knew.*

Zephyr took a few steps toward Era, one arm outstretched.

Era gave the message shipment to Chief Petroff without making eye contact and waited. Her muscles tensed, and her pulse thrummed in her ears. He would arrest her. Why else would Mali be looking at her like that?

The chief said something to Mali and strode away, message   to Dritan in one case,

Era's treasonous cube order addition in the other. She let her gaze follow him out the doors, and she exhaled when they slid shut behind him. He hadn't arrested her. They didn't know what she'd done.

But if they didn't know...

Zephyr grabbed Era's hand. Mali removed her eyepiece. She was crying.

Era looked from Mali to Zephyr and back.

A darkness bloomed within her, sucking her in, dragging her down. She took a step back, shaking her head. A moan rose in her throat and stuck there. Her intuition broke through, finally relaying the message it'd been sending since she first caught sight of Zephyr.

"I'm so sorry, child. There's been an accident on Soren."

CHAPTER FOURTEEN

As if a breach had opened, all air was sucked from the repository. Era pressed a fist to her chest, and Zephyr squeezed her other hand tighter.

"The report says there was a cave-in. No survivors." Mali's voice sounded far away, muffled like a damaged holovid.

"No," Era said. "No. Not his crew. I just got a message from him—"

"It was his crew." Mali's voice was firm, denying all hope.

"They need to keep looking, then. They have oxygen, ways to survive..." Era took a step toward Mali and tried to shake off Zephyr's grasp. "What did the message say?" Era's voice cracked at the end of her words.

169

Mali moved around the station and touched Era's arm. "Executive got the message yesterday. The accident happened three days ago."

"He could still be alive—"

"They've scanned the area of the cave-in and have detected no life."

"Tech can be wrong."

"It's been three days. And they don't report loss of life until they're certain. I'm sorry."

Era bent over, clutching her chest, the tiles beneath her blurring in and out of focus.

Three days. No sign of life.

Emergency supplies lasted two.

Punishment. Losing her husband, her baby defective, just like what happened to the traitor.

I'll never do anything wrong again. I'll be a model colonist, live quietly, not question things. Please let him be alive.

But who was listening?

The universe didn't care who lived and died. Soren had no say in it. People just died. They just did, and there was never a reason.

Her eyes burned, and her legs gave out beneath her. She crumpled to the cold floor. *I knew what would happen the day he left. I knew. I knew he'd never come back.*

A strangled sob made it past the pain in her throat, and hot tears slid down her cheeks. She drew her knees in to her chest and rocked back and forth, barely aware of Zephyr and Mali by her side, rubbing her neck, squeezing her arms, saying things she couldn't make out.

Era tasted the salt of her tears. She dropped her face onto her knees and wept.

He was never coming back.

"Get up, Era. Come on. Let's go back to your cubic." Zephyr pulled on her arm.

Era let Zephyr and Mali drag her to her feet. Mali handed her a suit scrap, and Era wiped uselessly at her nose, at the tears still streaming down her face.

"Take her back. Stay with her," Mali said.

Zephyr took Era's arm and led her to the repository doors. Everyone in the waiting area stared, but Era couldn't stop crying. The blackness had swallowed her. She didn't care what they thought. Let them see it.

Everyone had lost someone. Why'd they bury it, pretend it was all okay?

Until someone didn't. Like the traitor. He hadn't been able to live with what had been taken from him.

Could she?

Era pressed the wet scrap up to her mouth and allowed Zephyr to drag her down the stairs and through the corridors. People stepped out of the way and averted their eyes.

When they got to Era's cubic, she stood still, numb from the inside out. Zephyr gently removed Era's shift card from her pocket and opened the cubic. Era would have to move back to the singles sector now, back with Zephyr.

Zephyr activated the helio, illuminating the space, and Era stumbled to the bunk and collapsed onto it, the pain swelling in her again.

Never coming back.

She drew Dritan's pillow to her like she had every night since he'd gone. The scent of him was faint, but still there. She buried her face in it, and silent sobs wracked her body.

She heard Zephyr fumbling around on the shelf next to the bunk and felt a hand on her back.

"Drink some of this," Zephyr said.

Era sat up and took the canteen Zephyr offered her, but just cried harder. She bent over, clutching her belly.

Zephyr held up the clear package of pills. "They gave you grimp?"

172

Era nodded, and Zephyr squeezed one from the pack. "Take it."

"No." Era tried to catch her breath. "The president killed him. She killed Dritan. She's been lying to us about the Defect. They can save my baby."

She reached out and gripped Zephyr by the arm. "I recorded it all. So when I tell them I won't abort...if they arrest me for treason, you can get the recording and tell them what I know." The words came out halting, broken by her sobs.

Zephyr's brow wrinkled, and she hissed in a breath through her teeth. "I don't understand. What recording? What does this have to do with...with your abortion?"

"The Defect's a lie." Era choked on the words as they came. "I recorded the truth. Hid it. They won't take my baby."

"Recorded what? You think...you think the Defect is a lie? I know this is—take this. Take this. So we can talk." Zephyr held the tablet up to Era's lips.

Era turned her head. Hysteria was rising in her, a chaotic pulse of fear and panic mingling with her grief. Dritan was dead, and she'd soon follow him if she refused to get an abortion.

"You have to listen. The Defect—"

Zephyr pressed the tablet to Era's mouth, and Era clamped it shut and shook her head.

"It's not addicting unless you take it for a long time," Zephyr said softly. "It'll help. You need to calm down."

Era's whole body ached, and the walls of the cubic seemed to be moving closer, squeezing the air from the room, suffocating her.

The loss, the Dritan-shaped hole inside her felt like something she could never crawl out of. Zephyr pushed the tablet against Era's lips, more insistent now, and Era opened them. The pain would fade, just for a little while.

The pill dissolved on Era's tongue, and she took a sip of water to wash the bitter taste away. The drug would make it easier for Era to breathe, to talk and get Zephyr to listen.

Era sank back onto the bunk, tears still leaking from her eyes, and stared at the ceiling. Her distorted reflection stared back at her, and she watched her face relax as the drug took hold. Her hands unclenched, and a warm calm spread through her.

More of a numb- ness than calm, really.

It all just faded away, leaving her floating in an empty space where nothing mattered.

"I'm so sorry," Zephyr said.

Era's gaze shifted to Zephyr. She watched her take her eyepiece and handheld from her pocket and set them on the shelf.

"What do you want to tell me? About the Defect?"

"Play something for me." Her own voice sounded disembodied to her ears, as if it came from someone else's mouth.

"Play what?" Zephyr didn't meet Era's eyes.

"The song. The song you finally finished."

Zephyr nodded, and Era stared up at the ceiling again, her hands on her belly. Would the grimp harm her baby? She'd taken it without thinking. What did that say about her? About the grimp? She should feel anxious now, but she didn't. This drug erased everything. The tiny part of her that wanted to care rose up and floated away.

"I'm not aborting," Era said.

"Shh. Just relax. I'll play you the song."

"No. I'm a traitor." It sounded casual, like she'd said *I'm tired.*"

The music began to play, and Zephyr laid on the bunk. "Shh. Stop talking like that."

Era stared into Zephyr's blue eyes. "I love you, Zeph. You're the best friend anyone could ask for."

"I love you, too." Zephyr's voice sounded strained. "I'll stay with you 'til curfew, but I need to be back at my cubic for bunk check."

"I wish you could stay."

"I'll take your shift card with me, so I can let myself back in. I'll be back before first mess. Back before you even wake up." Tears spilled from Zephyr's eyes, tracking wet lines down her pale face.

"Don't cry," Era said. She smiled and wiped Zephyr's cheek with her hand. "You're the strong one."

Zephyr sniffed and snuggled up to Era, wrapping one pale arm around her. Era's mind whispered to her to tell Zephyr everything, but she was so tired. She could tell Zephyr the plan after night shift, couldn't she? There would still be time.

Era closed her eyes, and Zephyr's recorded voice rang out in the small space, enveloping them in the melody.

Hope's a dying star.
We need super-   nova.

To wipe space clean
And just start over.

There's more than this; I feel it.
Drifting through
this useless existence.

Held down
Held down
Held down
By artificial gravity.

Era closed her eyes, the music pulsing within her, and let the beat carry her away.

∞

Dark red liquid. Sticky, half-dry. The thick metallic scent of it fills my lungs, and my stomach heaves.
Blood coats the doors, drips down the number six. I'm on all fours, in a pool of it.
I scream and try to stand, but I'm sealed to the landing.
The doors to level six slide open, and I can't scream, can't even breathe. A hull breach.
But the doors shut. Air is restored to my lungs.

I pull against the floor again, and my hands come free. I run.

Up.

To Observation.

The deck is empty. Zephyr's not here.

It's just me.

Me and Soren.

Era opened her eyes. She'd never escaped the breach before in the nightmare.

A helio hovered in the air above, and she sat up, glancing around, disoriented. She was in her cubic. In her bunk, the blanket thrown off, her suit stuck to her sweat-covered body, her boots still tied on.

Her gaze landed on Dritan's shift card, hanging from its hook on the wall.

He's dead.

Her throat tightened, and she reached for the grimp packet and canteen on her shelf. She squeezed another pill onto her tongue and washed it down.

Her muscles relaxed, and a numb calm flowed through her, settling into her bones. She leaned against the wall, staring into nothing.

The sound of gears grinding brought her

out of it. She straightened, eyes riveted to the door.

It slid open, revealing a sole helio hovering in the corridor and darkness beyond.

Two men stepped into her cubic.

The silver infinity symbols on their sleeves glinted in the light. *Guards.*

Era stumbled to her feet.

The helio moved, illuminating their faces. Chief Petroff stood closest to her. Tadeo Raines, his face downturned, was behind him.

Chief Petroff stepped forward and grasped Era's arm. Her mind registered pain at his tight grip, but the pain felt dull, and so very far away.

"Era Corinth. You're under arrest for treason."

CHAPTER FIFTEEN

"No. I didn't do anything." Era tried to pull away from the chief.

They knew. But how did they know? She'd erased her eyepiece signature.

He gripped her tighter. "Where's your husband's shift card?"

Era's eyes darted to the hook, but she didn't answer him.

"Raines, over there. Get it."

Why did they want Dritan's shift card?

The chief pulled Era from her cubic, and she stumbled alongside him, struggling to keep up with his broad steps.

She shivered as they walked down the chill corridor. She'd never been any good at lying.

What made her think she could commit treason and get away with it?

Her mind knew these things. She could see her situation in a cold, detached way, as if her problems were a glitch in a piece of tech. She knew she should feel terrified, but she couldn't muster even a spark of fear. The grimp had stolen her emotions, left her with nothing but cool logic.

The corridor was silent, except for the thud of their boots hitting the tiles beneath their feet. Two pairs. No. Three. Tadeo had come up behind them.

They reached the stairwell, and Era expected them to take her upward, to executive sector. The breach on level six had been fixed a few days ago.

Only they didn't. They went down. Down to the sublevels, which held the machines that powered the ship, cleaned the air, and recycled the waste.

She should try to escape. But where would she run? There was nowhere to go. And running would be more proof of her guilt.

No. She had to maintain her innocence. She'd erased the evidence. They couldn't prove anyone had looked at the cube. They couldn't even prove anyone had added it to the list on purpose.

They took her down deep, deeper than she'd ever been. The hum of the power core grew, until she felt it through the soles of her boots. It was too loud down here, and the air, scorching. The hum grew to a dull roar as they descended.

When they reached level P2, Chief Petroff led them through a maze of corridors, never letting up on the tight grip he had on her arm.

They finally stopped at a cubic, and the chief swiped his card. The door slid open. He said something to Tadeo, but she couldn't hear it over the roar of the power core. How could anyone work down here?

The chief pushed her into the compartment, and the door slid closed behind her.

It was quieter in here, and she could hear her own rapid breathing. The tiny compartment looked like it'd been meant for storage, but the shelves had been ripped out, and the walls were covered in the same rubber floor tiles they used in the living cubics. Why were the walls padded with floor tiles?

A lume bar flickered above a single metal chair.

Era turned to face the door, waiting. Sweat trickled down her back, between her shoulder blades. She flexed her fingers. What were they going to do to her?

The door opened, and the roar intensified. Chief Petroff stepped through, a metal case in his grasp.

President Nyssa Sorenson walked in behind him. Her suit looked pressed and new, her blond hair smooth and tight in a low bun on her head. But the flickering lume bar above brought out the lines in her face and made her pale eyes appear sunken.

Era clenched her hands into fists and felt the first thing she'd felt since taking the grimp. Resentment. This woman had killed Dritan and wanted to kill her baby. This woman was lying to the entire fleet.

The door closed, and the hum died back down.

"Sit," the president said.

Era shook her head and took a step back.

The president sighed and met Era's eyes. "There are two ways we can do this. You can either sit and answer my questions honestly, or, if you'd prefer, we can use the drugs in that case to encourage you to answer hon-

184

estly."

Drugs. What drugs? Why had she never heard of this? Is this what they did to everyone they arrested? Uncertainty began to worm its way into her mind. The grimp wouldn't last forever. And some part of her brain understood she'd care about this, feel the danger more keenly once its effect faded.

"Why did you bring me here?" Era's voice came out strong. They couldn't possibly have proof of her guilt.

The president gestured to the chief, and he grabbed Era's arms and pushed her into the chair. He'd gotten long strips of scrap fabric from somewhere, and he forced her wrists down, strapping them to the armrests.

"I didn't do anything."

"Leave us," the president said.

Petroff hesitated, but left the cubic.

The president took a step closer to Era, her blue eyes narrowed.

Era pulled against the restraints. "Let me go. I didn't do anything."

"Did you think it would be that easy to erase your eyepiece signature from an archive cube? Didn't you realize there'd be backup data?"

Era froze and kept her face blank. *Of course.* Of course there would be a memory core backup. How could she be so stupid? The president wasn't bluffing. Era had made a sloppy, fatal mistake.

Mali had been banging on the door to storage, and Era hadn't thought to check, to search again. She licked her lips and struggled to keep her expression from giving away her guilt.

"So now, we have an archive cube with damaged files. And your eyepiece signature to go with them," the president said. "For a tech, you didn't try very hard to hide evidence of your treason."

Damaged files? When she'd used her father's trick to hack the memory core, she'd known it could damage it. "Which files?"

"So you admit to accessing the cube."

"Have *you* seen what's on it?" Era leaned forward, scrutinizing the president's face.

"Have you?"

"I asked first."

The president blinked. "What did you see on that cube, Era? If you don't tell me—"

"You'll...do what? Drug me? Did you drug

that half you took from the galley, too? If the fleet knew—"

"Tell me what you saw." The president drew each word out.

"Nothing. I didn't see anything." Era settled back in her chair and focused on the rubber tiles on the wall. *Soundproofing.* The tiles were there to keep the sound of the power core out. *No.* She straightened in her seat. They were there to keep the sound *in.*

"I don't believe you." The president faced the door and raised her fist. She paused and turned back to Era. "I think you should know. After these drugs enter your system, you'll no longer need an abortion. The cells will be terminated very soon after the first dose. But the aftermath will not be as easy as an abortion would've been."

Terminated. A flicker of fear burgeoned in Era's gut. "Wait."

"Yes?"

Her mind cycled through her options, listing and discarding them one by one. Did she have a choice? She could continue to lie and be drugged. Her baby would die. She could tell the truth and what? They'd convict her of treason. Her baby would die with her.

187

If she found a way to keep them from drugging her, she'd still be forced to get an abortion. Because she could never tell the medic what she knew, not after this.

She still had her fail-safe, but it was useless. She'd never even told Zephyr where to find it. Had Zephyr even been listening to what Era had said about the Defect?

That left...begging.

"I'll tell you what I saw," Era said. "But, just...please let my baby live."

"Your baby has the Defect. I have no control—"

"Babies with the Defect can be cured. My baby can live."

The president's face fell, and she turned her head partway away from Era. "We must use our resources for the healthy and the living," she said, her voice almost too quiet to make out over the low hum. "I wish you hadn't accessed those files. Truly, I do."

She took a deep breath, and her voice turned hard. "But accessing the archives is treason. You were training for archivist. You knew that better than anyone."

Era was falling, spiraling out of control.

The grimp was wearing off.

Her pulse quickened, and she pulled against her restraints. "Please. Just do the surgery. Let me have the baby. Save it. Then you can do whatever you want with me. I won't tell anyone—"

"I'm sorry. You've compromised the safety and peace of this fleet."

"I won't tell anyone." Era's voice cracked.

The president looked down at the floor. "The fleet won't ever know the archives were compromised."

"I have proof. If you do anything to me, everyone in the fleet will find out the truth."

President Sorenson's eyes widened, and she stared at Era. "You're lying."

"I'm not. You'll see." But Era was lying, because no one even knew where she'd hidden the proof. Her lie must have shown on her face. The president gave a slight shake of her head and turned to bang on the door.

Era laughed, and it sounded forced, too loud in the tight space. "Everyone will find out you've been lying about the Defect. And that you're expanding the subcity, and you arrest people and torture them. They'll turn against you. You won't win."

She sounded crazed, like Sam had in helio sector. How had she not seen how right he'd been?

The door opened, and the president said something to Chief Petroff before walking out. The chief removed Era's restraints and yanked her to her feet.

A bitter taste flooded Era's mouth. "Please, don't do this. Let me go back to my cubic. I won't say anything."

The chief grunted and pulled her into the corridor. Tadeo waited there, his eyes locked onto the floor. He didn't look up, didn't acknowledge her as she moved past.

Her limbs were weak, shaky, and the walls seemed to tilt around her. The chief half-carried, half-dragged her to the end of the corridor and took something from Tadeo. A shift card.

Not Tadeo's. He still had his hooked to his belt.

Dritan's shift card.

They'd planned this from the moment they'd arrested her.

The chief swiped the card, and the door opened. He pulled her across the threshold.

A control panel and a pane of glass

was all that separated them from the bare metal space beyond.

The maintenance airlock.

CHAPTER SIXTEEN

Era's survival instincts kicked in. She ripped her arm from the chief's grasp and backed into Tadeo.

He pushed her forward, and Petroff slammed a hand across her face. She stumbled against the wall and sank to her knees.

The control panel went in and out of focus, but the sting of the blow shocked her awake.

She was going to die.

"Tadeo." Era stumbled to her feet. She reached for his arm, but he backed up a step, avoiding her gaze and her reach.

Chief Petroff looked from Era to Tadeo and back. "You know this traitor?"

Tadeo's nostrils flared. "No."

Era lunged toward the door, but the chief grabbed her by the back of her suit and held her as she struggled against him. Cold, hard metal pressed against her temple, and she froze.

"I can just pulse you now," he said. "But I'd rather not have a mess to clean up. Strip her, Raines. Can't waste a good suit."

Era's stomach churned, but she stayed still. Was there any way out?

Tadeo unlaced her boots and took them off. Then he stood and gripped the zipper on her suit. A sheen of sweat coated his forehead, and one fat drop traced a slow trail down his brow.

He unzipped her suit.

Tears gathered in Era's eyes, and a hard lump expanded in her throat. "Don't do this, Tadeo, please," she whispered.

The chief released her and forced her sleeves off her arms, ripping the suit away. It fell to the floor, and the cold air hit her sweat-soaked skin. Goosebumps lifted along the length of her body. She wrapped her arms across her exposed breasts and whimpered, shame flooding her. The chief pressed the pulse gun's icy barrel against her neck.

Tadeo's eyes flicked from her

swollen belly to the chief. "We can't..." he said, his voice rough.

"It's Defective," the chief said. "Set to be aborted tomorrow. She tampered with the archives, erased data we need to settle on a new Earth. She knew the penalty."

"No! I didn't erase anything. I didn't mean to. I just had to know the truth." Era's voice shook. "My baby—"

The barrel pressed harder into Era's skin, silencing her.

"But Chief, sir—"

"Raines." The chief's voice was hard, edged with unspoken threat.

Tadeo threw his shoulders back in the conditioned response of one trained to respond to commands without thought. But his eyes darted, wary, between Era and the chief, and his hands were balled into tight fists. A glimmer of hope burgeoned in Era's chest. Tadeo took a step forward.

The chief dropped the pulse gun from Era's neck and pushed her away. She stumbled to the side and hit her arm hard on the control panel. She cradled it against her bare breasts as the chief walked up to Tadeo and stopped an inch from his face. Tadeo didn't back down.

"Remember McGill?" the chief asked. "They told you all he went back to his home deka. Sent back 'cause he couldn't handle the shame of a traitor nearly killing Tesmee with *his* pulse gun."

Tadeo stood straighter, his jaw working.

The chief lifted the pulse gun and gestured with it. "McGill was in on it...He was working with that traitor to kill Tesmee." His voice rose. "He gave that traitor his pulse gun. I airlocked him myself. Fleet doesn't need to know we had a traitor in the guard. I'd do it again if I thought, even for a second, we had other traitors in the guard. Do you understand?"

Tadeo's eye twitched, and he slowly nodded.

Era let out a small moan and looked toward the door. She had to get away. The chief pointed the pulse gun at her and gestured to the door that led into the airlock. Era took a few hesitant steps toward it, her gaze shifting between Tadeo and the chief.

"Activate it. It's got to look like she did it," Petroff said.

Era's lips parted as Tadeo passed Dritan's shift card over the control panel. *Zephyr will believe I committed sui- cide. She won't even question it. She'll think I killed myself because Dritan died and because they were taking my baby.*

The fail-safe might've worked. Why didn't I try harder to get her to listen?

Tadeo pressed a button, and the alarms sounded.

Era reached toward Tadeo. "They're lying to all of us about the Defect."

The chief pressed the pulse gun into her temple. "Open the door."

Tadeo hesitated, but swiped Dritan's shift card across the scanner.

"No, wait. My baby can survive. Please, let me have the baby. I don't care what you do with me after that. I have proof. I can show you. They can save the baby—"

Chief Petroff shoved Era into the airlock. She twisted, trying to get back into the control room, but the door slid closed, nearly trapping her fingers.

She straightened, teeth chattering from the frigid air, and turned to face them. The alarms blared, deafening, echoing off the metal walls of the airlock. She held one hand over the swell of her belly and banged the other against the glass. "Don't do this! My baby can be saved. I won't tell anyone!"

The chief watched her with his arms crossed, an impassive expression on his face. Tadeo stood beside him, clenching and un-clenching his fists, but didn't move to help her.

The grimp was gone.

Era began to hyperventilate as she banged the glass, over and over, until Tadeo turned his face away.

Would she feel herself dying?

When the airlock opened, she'd be swept into space, the air stolen from her lungs. Her bones would crack in the cold, and she'd spend her last moments of consciousness with nothing between her and the angry red planet that had stolen so much. *Soren.*

Chief Petroff and Tadeo blurred before her, and she used one hand to wipe the tears from her cheeks.

She rested both palms against the swell of her belly.

I'm so sorry I couldn't save you.

The old Earth religions taught about life af-ter death. But those gods never existed. There was only alive or dead. Breathing or not breathing. At least now she wouldn't have to live without Dritan and their baby.

She began to count the rivets in the floor, pushing down her panic. How long until the airlock opened?

The alarm blared louder, and its pace quickened.

No. Her last image could not be of this ship.

Era lifted her wrist and focused on her infinity tattoo. She took a deep sputtering breath and closed her eyes.

Dritan. The curves of his well-muscled body, his high cheekbones, his full lips. The feeling of his strong, warm arms around her, and his hazel eyes looking into hers. *Safe.*

He'd come to her after his shift that day, two weeks after the riots. He'd washed and pressed his grease-stained sublevel suit, had tried to clean up, look good for her.

He'd run a hand through his dark curls, pulling on them, so nervous to ask the question he'd come to ask.

"*I want to come back to you every night,*" he'd said. "*I want to be paired with you. Do you want that, too?*"

Yes.

The portal groaned behind her.

Era swept into space, the air stolen from her lungs, her bones cracking in pain from the frigid cold.

Her eyes adjusted, and she saw the stars.

Beautiful, twinkling against the vast expanse. Sparkling promises of a better world waiting.

Darkness closed in around the edges of her vision, and the stars blinked out.

PARAGON: BOOK TWO OF LEGACY CODE

The dangers in the fleet are growing, and the Paragon Guard is called upon to keep the colonists safe. Tadeo Raines struggles with his role in recent events and must finally come to terms with the dark secret he's been running from...

Please visit **AutumnKalquist.com** to learn more about Legacy Code, and subscribe to the newsletter for updates.

LEGACY CODE SOUNDTRACK

Autumn Kalquist and music producer Freya Wolfe have created an official soundtrack for Legacy Code.

Please visit **AutumnKalquist.com** to find out how you can listen to "Artificial Gravity", the song featured in this book.

"ARTIFICIAL GRAVITY" LYRICS

A straight line
from first breath to last.
This recycled air remembers
all the lies told in its past.

Sins of the father,
that's what they say.
That's how life goes,
what we're living today.

There's more than this; I feel it.
Drifting through
this useless existence.
Held down

Held down
Held down
By artificial gravity.

Blinded by tradition,
I slept, like those before.
But now I see the truth,
I'm awake, and I want more.

There's more than this; I feel it.
Drifting through
this useless existence.
Held down
Held down
Held down
By artificial gravity.

Hope's a dying star.
We need a supernova.
To wipe space clean,
And just start over.

There's more than this; I feel it.
Drifting through
this useless existence.
Held down

Held down
Held down
By artificial gravity

FRACTURED ERA SERIES

DEFECT

DEFECT: PART ONE
DEFECT: PART TWO
DEFECT: PART THREE
DEFECT: PART FOUR

LEGACY CODE

LEGACY CODE
PARAGON

ACKNOWLEDGMENTS

So many people helped make this story what it is. I'd like to thank all my friends and family who jumped in and brainstormed with me or offered opinions about this book when I asked. Your support means a lot to me, and this book is better because of you.

Thanks to my beta readers, who gave me amazing feedback every step of the way: Jennifer Nelson, Marcos Romero, David Heringer, Kristen Ervin, MJ Colucci, and Scott Pritchard.

Erynn Newman, thank you for being an awesome editor and a joy to work with.

To Freya Wolfe, thank you for all those hours spent analyzing my plot, managing "the talent", and for believing in my vision and seeing it too.

A special thanks to Sita Payne Romero, Jamie Blair, and my husband, Juan, for the many hours you spent in my world with me. You're my brainstorming team, my alphas and betas, and you help me shape my stories in ways I could never do on my own.

And to my dad, Gregory Nelson, thank you for always believing in me and supporting me, no matter what.

CPSIA information can be obtained at www.ICGtesting.com
Printed in the USA
LVOW07s2019230415

435823LV00006BA/677/P

9 780615 982793